Looking Over My Shoulder

A Collection of Short Stories

by Harry Tomlin

Eloquent Books
New York, New York

Copyright 2007 by C. Harry Tomlin
All rights reserved.

No part of this book may be reproduced or transmitted in any form or by any means, graphic, electronic, or mechanical, including photocopying, recording, taping, or by any information storage retrieval system, without the permission, in writing, from the publisher.

Eloquent Books
An imprint of Writers Literary & Publishing Services, Inc.
845 Third Avenue, 6th Floor – 6016
New York, NY 10022
www.eloquentbooks.com

ISBN/SKU: 0-9795935-2-2
ISBN: 978-0-9795935-2-9
Library of Congress Control Number:

Printed in the United States of America

Wood carvings and chapter photos by Harry Tomlin
Book Design: Mark Bredt
Cover ©: Maxim Golubchikov / www.dreamstime.com

SHORT STORIES BY HARRY TOMLIN

A Prince of a Frog -- 3

Confession to my Little Brother -- 8

Dying for Love -- 15

Things I Don't Know -- 19

Ancient Tragedy – 33

Alaskan Adventure -- 38

Lucky Sister-in-Law -- 46

Guardian Angels -- 53

Hypnotized Sister -- 58

Talking Catbird -- 64

Mother Nature's Desires -- 70

Butternut Trees or Roses -- 75

Herbal Magic -- 79

Tribute to Dad -- 86

Family Ghost Stories – 89

My Korean Dilemma – 97

I Met Bigfoot – 104

Just Outside Roswell – 112

Birth of a Cynic – 122

Three Eagles Screaming -- 133

INTRODUCTION

Fourteen years ago, I became a paraplegic. My previously active life was drastically curtailed. I never took the time to try writing before I became disabled, though I always wanted to be an author. I have been writing short stories for several years now. My perspective is from a wheel chair, looking over my shoulder at what once was and what might have been.

Most of my short stories are fictional but I have them occurring in real environments and describing real adventures from my past life. They are a blend of the real and the surreal. My technique is to recall a time in my past life and ask myself, "what if?" Then I proceed to write what happened but with a little twist of reality.

Five of my short stories are not twisted and record actual events in my life. The stories named "Alaskan Adventure," "Birth of a Cynic," " Dying for Love," "Tribute to Dad" and "Three Screaming Eagles" give all true accounts.

The story named "Family Ghost Stories" may be fiction, since all ghost stories are suspect. I did not originate any of the ghost stories. I reported them here as family members, now departed, told them to me.

I cannot vouch for the truth of the events I read about and described in "Things I Don't Know." I do believe they happened but I could never prove they actually occurred.

A PRINCE OF A FROG

You see me now as a frog. Long ago, my name was Eagle Flying and I was a member of the Cherokee Indian Tribe. I lived in the Appalachian Mountains about 500 years ago, in the area now known as West Virginia.

A son of our tribal Chief, I was a proud young man. I had great physical strength and was a good hunter. Everything was easy for me and perhaps I was spoiled. I can admit now I was unkind to those less gifted.

In the fall of my 22nd year, I went on our tribe's big bear and deer hunt. I want to tell you now what happened on a hunt that changed my life forever.

Fighting Dog was my older brother and the leader of our hunting party. I resented him and often questioned his plans for hunting. He became irritated with me and ordered me to go hunt in a different place from he and his group of men.

This meant I would be alone until I could kill a bear or deer to take home. I was not at all pleased with this turn of events. Promising myself to kill a larger animal than anyone in my brother's party, I went hunting alone.

I saw several deer and bear in the following days but none was of exceptional size. I wandered many miles up the river by which we lived. I walked so far I was in the territory of a different tribe. I knew it was the territory of a tribe not friendly to my people.

The sixth day of my hunt was when the strange thing happened. I was walking on the crest of a ridge just above the river when I came upon a large grove of walnut trees. I heard some women talking as I approached. Soon I saw an old crone of a woman with a young girl of great beauty.

I watched them for some time from hiding. They were not from my tribe and I had never seen them before. They were gathering black walnuts. The girl was pleasing to my eyes and I became focused on her as I watched. I decided I must have this beautiful young woman. Because there was no one there to stop me, I walked to where both were and spoke to the girl.

They became startled and were on the point of running away. I told the girl I was going to have her sexually and asked if she would agree to my doing so. The old woman screeched threats of casting a spell on me if I did not leave. I grabbed the girl and tried to undress her while she fought me.

Out of the corner of my eye, I could see the old woman pouring some powder from a small gourd container on one of the walnuts. I was too preoccupied to know, or care, what she was doing.

The girl then twisted out of my grasp and started running away. I had just started after her when it happened. The old woman threw the walnut on which she had poured the powder. The walnut hit me on the side of my head.

The moment of impact was the last moment I had as a

man in a man's body.

I was still much aware of everything going on, but I was inside the walnut; indeed, I had become the walnut. I rolled a few feet and was aware of the old woman as she explained to her student how she had cast a spell and made me part of the walnut.

All of this happened more than 300 years ago. I have become comfortable with my new existence as just a consciousness. Having no body to be concerned with has its benefits.

I am aware of everything happening on this world. I am the ultimate observer. I do believe it has improved my character to watch and listen for five hundred years to the futile actions and exalted words of so many short-lived men and women.

Are you curious about how I came to be as you see me?

I was lucky and squirrels or other animals did not eat me. I grew into a magnificent black walnut tree on the top of the mountain ridge with a view of the whole world. I towered to the sky and thrived there for more than 500 years.

My serenity was lost when men clearing a path to install a new power line cut me down. I was terrified and it disrupted my sense of existence to lose my home atop the beautiful mountain. I feared that my tree would lie there on the mountain and soon completely decay. What would happen to my existence when the walnut tree was gone?

Thankfully, the man who owned the land recognized the value of walnut wood and brought me to his home.

Since I was aware of everything, I knew the man who owned me had a brother who used only hardwoods from which to carve. I decided to try and subtly influence the man to give some of my tree to his brother, so I might have some form for my consciousness to occupy. I could influence people because I had the ability to implant thoughts in their mind and convince them it was their idea. Unfortunately, this only worked for someone very near me. Just imagine what I might have done if my influence worked on distant people. I could have changed history!

I was successful and the disabled brother received a large chunk of my walnut wood. I went with the wood, or perhaps it would be more accurate to say, I went *in* it.

I knew my new owner had carved some noble creatures, such as horses, fish and birds. I was optimistic of taking the eagle form so my appearance will match my name, Eagle Flying.

The man who was deciding my future shape worked very slowly and for only a few hours a day. He first carved the box on the bottom while I anticipated anxiously what form he would carve on top. All the creatures he had previously carved were noble animals, so I had reason to be hopeful.

Finally, the day arrived that my benefactor started to carve the rough shape of what I was to look like for evermore. I still hoped he would carve a beautiful eagle, or at least a handsome horse.

Alas, it was not to be. He chose to carve a frog. *A frog!*

I see myself as the most noble of earth's creatures! For me to appear before the world as a *frog* is a terrible disgrace! I wanted revenge!

My conscience would not allow me to kill a human. The worst I could do to him was to influence his mind in a way that resulted in a crippling accident. However, alas, he frustrated me again. This man was already a cripple!

Since I am a most wise and sagacious being, I reversed my strategy. I would have this carver of wood write my life story. I would accept his glorification of me in lieu of my revenge on him. Therefore, that is how you come to be reading this tale. I will understand if you wish to worship the carving of my humble self.

CONFESSION TO MY LITTLE BROTHER

Most of us remember little of our early childhood. Only those events arousing strong and deep emotions stick in our memory many years later. Just such a series of events happened to me and I want to tell you about it here.

A beautiful spring morning when I was eight years old found me eager for adventure. This day I so vividly remember was a Saturday in May of 1946. My family was always busy on Saturday mornings doing the work postponed because of school and work during the previous week. Mom had not yet assigned any chores to me on this day. Being anxious to avoid that possibility, I set off to explore the hills surrounding my old home place in rural West Virginia.

My family's home sat on twenty-six acres at the head of a deep hollow between mountain ridges. A small creek flowed down the hollow by our home. A year-round spring of water fed from deep under the mountain and we carried it in buckets to the house for drinking. Mom used water from the creek to wash our clothes in a washtub with a scrubbing board. There was no electricity available there so we used kerosene lamps for lighting the nighttime. In retrospect, the worst hardship was going to the outdoor toilet at night in wintertime. Many of our neighbors lived with the same conditions in that time and place.

There was one-half mile of dirt road from my home to the nearest paved highway. The creek in our hollow crossed the dirt road three times between the main highway and home. After heavy rains, it was difficult for a small boy to walk this road and keep his feet dry. When walking to catch the bus for school after heavy rains, I learned to stop at each creek crossing, remove my shoes and roll up my pants legs, wade across creek and then replace my socks and shoes. I did not consider this a problem and enjoyed wading the swollen creek.

I started my adventure, that long ago Saturday, by walking along the dirt road toward a place where cattle-bars blocked the road. There I climbed the embankment by the roadside and proceeded to the top of the ridge.

Tree leaves were starting to bud but were not large enough as yet to block my view. I viewed the beautiful country surrounding the mountain ridge and was proud to call it home. After enjoying the scenery for a while, I decided to climb to the highest peak of this ridge, which the local people called Old Baldy. There was, and I suppose still is, a large boulder resting on the peak of Old Baldy. This rock had ledges on one side that made it possible to ascend to its top. I proceeded to climb the large stone to get a better view, since its top was the highest point around for as far as I could see.

There were chipmunks running everywhere in the woods that day. When I saw movement in the leaves on top of the boulder, I assumed it was another chipmunk and decided to try to catch it. I wanted a chipmunk for a pet.

I pounced on the spot where I had seen movement, scooped up leaves with both hands and eased open my hands to view the animal. To my surprise, it was not a chipmunk but a baby bird.

Looking up, I could see the nest from which it had fallen. It was on a tree limb extending over the boulder and was just above my head. I wanted to return the bird to its nest if I could but the nest was about two feet beyond my reach.

Plentiful loose stones lay all about this area. I proceeded to carry them, one at a time, to the top of the boulder. I stacked them to form a makeshift ladder beneath the bird's nest. When I was able to reach the nest from the pile of stones, I retrieved the baby bird from my shirt pocket and returned it to nest with its three siblings.

I was sitting on my stack of rocks taking a rest when I heard someone climbing up the boulder. This was only a little surprising since my older brother, several cousins and a few neighbors often roamed about in these mountains near our home.

The head and shoulders I could now see, however, belonged to no one I knew and I knew everyone for miles around. This visitor's head was heart shaped with pale skin. He had no nose but just two nostril holes where a nose should have been. When he finished climbing up and stood on top of the boulder, I could see he was only a little taller than I was. I would have liked to run home then but he was blocking my only escape path from the rock. I was a little scared because I had no idea who or what this thing before me was or what he wanted from me.

I was not aware of the stories of aliens visiting this planet when this happened. Even so, I could tell that my visitor was not like anyone I had ever met in my life.

My visitor spoke to me in a high-pitched voice, which sounded little different from my own. He said, "I greet the young human who is kind to baby birds."

I was shy as a child and had great difficulty talking to strangers, so when I did not reply, he sat down and talked to me for some time. I do not recall all he said but I will tell you what I remember.

My strange visitor reported, "Me and my family are studying your family and all the living things in this area. We want to learn your nature and how you survive. We come from a distant world and came here to learn about your planet."

The stranger's large eyes were deep and peaceful and I soon became less fearful.

"My family has performed many tests and experiments here to determine how you are like us and how you are different," he said.

I had noticed he was carrying a bag with a strap over his shoulder. Now he removed something from it and set it on the rock in front of me. I saw a small wooden box, which he then opened, and we viewed the contents. The box contained three glass tubes, two filled with a reddish powder and the other with some substance I could not identify.

My visitor then asked, "Will you do something for me?" I would have done anything to get away from him, so I nodded, yes.

"I have done a bad thing. I have disobeyed my parents and begun an experiment they will not allow me to finish," he disclosed. "My father ordered me to destroy it. I really do not want to lose it but father and mother will not allow me to keep it. Will you help me by finishing my experiment so it will not die?" I nodded my agreement to do this favor for him.

He replaced each of the three tubes back in the box and told me exactly what I was to do. Handing me the box, he said good-bye, quickly descended the boulder and walked away. I waited for a few minutes to be sure he was really gone before starting down the mountain for home.

Everyone was still busy at home and had not noticed my absence. I proceeded to start what was now my experiment. My visitor on the mountain had told me I would need a container for two gallons of water. I looked in our storage cellar built into the side of the mountain and found a two and one-half gallon water bucket my Dad used for gardening.

The Alien told me everything I used must be clean so I took the bucket to the nearby creek, scrubbed it with sand, and filled it with water. I needed a place to hide it and decided a corner of the cellar behind some boxes would be perfect, since no one looked there for long periods.

Following my visitor's instructions, I dumped the contents of one test tube, which had a small glob of fleshy appearing stuff, into the water. I added one tube of the red powder substance, just as instructed. The red powder was supposed to start the growth process. My instructions were to add the second tube of powder in three weeks. I placed a short length of wooden board over the bucket, stacked several empty gunnysacks on top and around the bucket and left it well concealed from my family.

As might be expected from any eight year old, I became impatient for something to happen. I checked the water bucket after school for the first three or four days. Not much was happening in the bucket so I lost interest.

My school was finished for the year and I had begun my summer vacation before I next remembered the experiment. When I went again to the cellar, the flesh blob had really grown. It now looked somewhat like a human baby. There was an odd-looking tube about six inches long coming out of its belly. At the end of this tube was a small round ball of flesh, which was contracting like a heartbeat. I guessed it must have been pumping the water/powder mixture inside the creature to feed it. I dumped the last tube of powder inside the bucket and hid it back in the corner. I was pleased with how the experiment was now growing.

I went into the house and checked a calendar to see if three weeks had passed. I was three days late adding the last tube of powder. Twenty-four days instead of twenty-one days must have been close enough, since it was still living.

Building a dam in the creek by our house for a swimming pool was a project my older brother and I took on every summer. We carried many rocks and stacked them to block the creek. Our dam leaked badly, so we had to shovel a lot of dirt on it to make it retain water. The swimming pool project and playing in the pool occupied me for the next two weeks.

The final week for the experiment was an anxious time for me. It was supposed to hatch very soon and I did not know how to keep it alive. I was thinking the alien kid must have been super dumb not to tell me how to tend to this thing after it hatched. My daily inspection showed it was alive and moving around more each day. The water level was down to about an inch in the bottom of the bucket by this time. My experiment looked almost exactly like a real baby. The only difference was the tube and ball extending from its stomach.

Then my secret experiment was exposed.

I did not notice my Mother hanging clothes to dry in our back yard when I went to check on the experiment the next day. When I removed the bucket from the corner and exposed it to the bright light the thing started crying. I thought it was screaming loudly for attention. I did not know what to do! I cradled it in my arms as I had seen others do with crying babies.

Mom could always hear everything you did not want her hear. Immediately she was by my side, and took the crying thing from my arms.

Talking about something hard to explain! Mom and Dad never did believe my story about the Alien. They thought I had found the baby somewhere nearby not long before they first saw the creature. In any event, they decided to keep it and raise it as one of their own. Mom felt sure some unwed mother had abandoned it, even though no one ever reported any missing babies in our community.

This is the true story of how you came into this world, my little brother. Please forgive me for neglecting you while you grew in the bucket. You may wonder, as I do, if you have any genes from the Aliens. Do you ever feel otherworldly?

DYING FOR LOVE

I was recently thinking about the various types of love people experience when I remembered a young man who died for the greatest, and perhaps least understood, of all loves.

The love between a parent and child is the first we encounter. Except for a few exceptions which are probably always due to a mental illness, the parent/child love is so prevalent it could be said to be instinctive. This love is not dependent on anything other than the biological fact of the parent/child relationship. Parent/child love is strong and continues even after cases of physical or mental abuse. This defies logical reasoning; therefore, this love must be instinctive.

The type of love most celebrated in literature, song and cinema is romantic love. Instinct is also the primary cause of this love.

When men and women have grown enough of their glands to start producing hormones, they develop an overwhelming interest in the opposite sex. The urge to mate is the prime consideration in nearly everything they say or do.

When they are old enough to mate and get married, they usually follow a predictable search method to locate a partner of the opposite sex.

They direct their love like a beam of light into the dark night. If any potential partner acts as a mirror and reflects the light of love back, it grows and often results in life-long relationships. If the potential mate does not reflect love back, the light beam dims and soon goes dark. Then the love beam moves on to another in this ritual search.

Some go through many relationships before finding one strong enough to last. Others never find a "true love" partner in this strange human game.

Love of friends and family members may be the most reasonable type of love. This love in not instinctive but derives from common interests and shared experiences. No demands are made of the loved ones. Loving friends and relatives can do the most to make our lives happy.

The type of love which makes heroes is the one of which I will speak here. This greatest of emotions is glorified and best exemplified by those who are willing to die, and do die, for those they love.

Most of us are astounded who witness or hear of the bravery and depth of love that causes heroes to voluntarily give up their life. A person volunteering to die in an attempt to help others stands as the ultimate expression of ones love of humanity.

There have been many examples of this special love. We hear of attempts to save a drowning victim by someone who cannot swim; thus drowning himself or herself. Some of these heroes have run into a burning, collapsing building to save someone. They had to know their chance of survival was next to nothing.

Wartime conditions have produced most of our heroes. Many military men have gone willingly to their deaths for love of their fellowman. In each of the Wars of the last one hundred years, several soldiers placed themselves on top of a live grenade and died to save nearby companions.

There have been many men in wartime choosing to die to save others lives. I knew one of these heroes. His name was Darrel.

The year was 1951. The news told of the conflict in Korea. Dad and I were working at trimming undergrowth by the roadside in front of our home. Four local young men came by and asked Dad for advice about enlisting in the military to fight in Korea.

My Dad was in the First World War and he had three sons in World War II, so they considered him an expert on such matters. (He later had another son in Korea and his two youngest sons in Vietnam.)

My father talked with the young men for some time. He told them, "Many people die and suffer in all wars. If you are in a war zone, you will endure and witness many terrible things. If you are not able to accept the possibility of dying there, I advise you not to go to Korea.

"The only reason we now live in freedom is many young men fought and died to preserve our freedom. I believe if men anywhere are in a fight for their freedom, we should volunteer our help. Everyone's freedom is at risk when some people are not free."

Three of the four young men enlisted in the military. Two of the three eventually came home, but Darrel was lost in action.

The Chinese army pushed into South Korea and overran many American and allied positions. Darrel's unit had to retreat when the Chinese Army was nearly on top of them. Darrel held his position and fired a machine gun at the enemy. He alone held up the Chinese advance just enough to allow most of his unit to retreat from certain destruction. Darrel died because of his heroic effort that day. The U. S. Army never found Darrel's body.

Fifty-five years later in 2006, local people in North Korea while digging a ditch found a mass grave. A special investigative team was able to identify Darrel's remains with a DNA test. This hero finally came home.

I read of Darrel's burial in a local newspaper from where we lived back then. Many local people besides Darrel's remaining family members attended his funeral. The homecoming of this forgotten hero brought a tear to my eye.

I remain in awe of Darrel, who loved so much he gave all he had – his life.

THINGS I DON'T KNOW

Human knowledge of our world and the universe has made great advances in the last few centuries. The learning process has a snowball effect, with more understanding gained in the last 100 years than in all our preceding history. Our scientists now understand the intricate workings of many processes of nature and can manipulate some of them.

Many knowledgeable scientists and medical researchers believe mankind will someday be able to understand and manipulate all matter by building on the present knowledge base. I sincerely hope they are right. I do have doubts they can reach their goals without understanding many strange events they are now ignoring.

While most things are understandable by applying present scientific techniques, other things exist on a different level. These oddities are beyond understanding by investigative methods used today. When scientists confront one of these mysteries contradicting their established laws of nature, they ignore it.

Modern science sets the paradigm for study within the limits of the senses of sight, hearing, smell, feel, and taste. Most scientists believe these five senses are the only human tools we can use to gain knowledge. Parapsychologists dare to look outside these parameters but the mainstream scientists often discredit their studies.

I will discuss here some of the strange phenomena that have been observed and recorded but ignored by scientists.

Any basic study of the human brain will inform you it is capable of much more than we normally use. These studies indicate our sub-conscious mind remembers everything we detect by our five senses.

Scientists have stimulated recall in an 85-year-old man by placing special electrodes in the parts of his brain that control memory. His memory while being stimulated was vastly more specific than his normal memory. He quoted verbatim a newspaper article read a half-century earlier.

The brain has incredible complexity and power and can process millions of pieces of information per second. The conglomeration of billions of neurons and hundreds of billions of interconnections are slightly different in each human brain. This brain difference is the physical reason each of us is a unique person.

The brain has two distinct modes or levels of functioning. These modes are named the conscious state and the sub-conscious state. Most of us can only operate at the conscious level except for when we dream or are hypnotized. A few people claim they can use their sub-conscious state to learn things thought to be impossible. There are enough documented cases to strongly suggest that the brain, under the proper circumstances, can have knowledge of what is happening in far distant places and sometimes, even what will happen in the future.

The people who are able to do these things must have a pathway between their conscious and sub-conscious. A very few people have proven they are able to consult with their subconscious minds to a very limited extent.

Many people today claim to be psychics and say they can see the future. Investigations have proven nearly all are fakes. The few who seem legitimate are accurate only occasionally. A psychic ability seems to be a freak of nature that may happen a few times with some people, and very rarely and with a very few, is under their control. It is a spontaneous event and totally unplanned. I believe that if we would expend more time and energy studying the ESP phenomena, it might be possible someday for humans to exist at an entirely different level. I will call it a spiritual level for lack of a better term.

Dreams sometimes enable the dreamer to ignore time and distance, with results which are in violation of the concepts of conventional science. One such dream happened to a reporter for the Boston Globe newspaper in 1883.

Reporter Ed Samson awoke on a couch in the newsroom of the Boston Globe after sleeping off a binge. Samson awoke with a clear recall of a very frightening dream. In his dream, he saw molten rock pouring down a mountainside and over people and small towns. An incredible explosion sent the island up in a column of fire and then the boiling seawaters rushed into the space where the island had been.

Being a writer, Samson wrote down the details of his dream in case it might someday be of use and left it on his desk. His notes said the island was Pralape, a little island near Java in the south pacific.

The editor found Ed Samson's notes the next morning and mistook it for a story from over the telegraph wires. He ran it as a front-page story for august 29, 1883. Later, when he could find no confirmation of the story, he talked to Ed Samson. Samson admitted it came from his dream.

The editor fired Ed Samson. He was preparing to write a retraction for Samson's story when reports came trickling in of a great disaster somewhere in the pacific. In a few days, all the newspapers were reporting the island of Krakatau had totally disappeared in a volcanic eruption at the exact time of Samson's dream.

Samson's dream was very accurate in detail except for the island's name. He used Pralape for Krakatau. Several years later, the Danish historical society sent Samson an old map that showed the natives called the island Pralape. The name Pralape had not been used for the Island in more than 150 years.

Another well documented case of a person using the trance state for his benefit centers around the death of the famous writer, Charles Dickens.

Charles Dickens had started to write his first attempt at a mystery story when he died in 1870. He named the story "The Mystery of Edwin Drood." He contracted to write twelve chapters for a magazine who was to publish a chapter monthly. He had completed only six chapters when he died.

A young printer named Thomas P. James came to Brattleboro, Vermont within the year after dickens died. He rented a room from a lady who believed in spiritualism, then widely accepted. He attended a number of sittings in his landlady's parlor at which the customary trances and rapping occurred. Then, on October 3, 1872, he informed his landlady that he had been in contact with the spirit of Charles Dickens and the author had given him power of attorney to complete the unfinished novel, "The Mystery of Edwin

Drood."

Witnesses later testified that James would go to his room, slump in his chair and go into trances that often lasted for hours. Afterward, he would write the next lines of the mystery. He explained to friends that he was creating nothing, merely writing down what Dickens had told him in the trance.

When word of what he was doing leaked out, all the newspapers called it a fraud and a hoax. Less than a year later, the finished manuscript was printed and appeared in the bookstalls. Even the experts said that it sounded exactly like it should if Dickens had written it. A Boston paper wrote that James could not have written this book without help from Dickens.

Sir Arthur Conan Doyle, the creator of Sherlock Holmes, investigated the strange case of Thomas James. Doyle reported that James showed no literary talent before or after this one manuscript. James education ended at age thirteen after the fifth grade. Doyle said he could not distinguish the last chapters from the first part written by Dickens before his death.

Thomas James never wrote again and died in obscurity.

Another strange story is told about a man named Arthur Stilwell. He became wealthy building railroads at the time they were expanding in this country. Stilwell started with nothing, unlike the railroad barons of New York. This man amassed a fortune, and even found his wife, by listening to voices in his head. Stilwell claimed the voices occurred in his sleep and sometimes while he was sitting by a lamp trying to read.

The voices told Stilwell to build a connecting railroad

between the wheat fields of Kansas and the shipping ports on the Gulf of Mexico. Time after time, when problems faced him, he would go to his office, pull the shades and ask for guidance from the voices. All went well until he was 50 miles from Galveston, Texas, which was his intended termination.

The voices told him that Galveston was doomed and not to have his railroad end there. His business partners and the people of Galveston were furious. Stilwell stuck to his change of plans and the railroad terminated at a desolate spot on the coast. This new terminal became Port Arthur, Texas after Stilwell's first name. Then, as history reports, a hurricane devastated Galveston but left Port Arthur untouched.

Stilwell wrote a book in 1910 that reported in detail the coming of WWI. He wrote another book in 1914 reporting on all the war details and the results.

Arthur Stilwell died in 1928 so there was at least one problem the voices could not help him resolve. His wife stepped out of Manhattan skyscraper window two weeks after his death.

Next, I will tell you a story of reincarnation from India. Shanti Devi was born to middle class parents in Delhi, India in 1926. When she was seven years old, she told her mother that she had lived before in a town called Muttra. The parents took the child to a physician and he could find no mental problems. She persisted in saying she had lived before. The doctor advised the parents to keep a log of what she said.

Shanti Devi claimed, in nineteen hundred and thirty-five, to have been married and given birth to three children in a previous life. She described her children and gave their names. Her name in the previous life had been Ludgi, she said. The parents were convinced that Shanti was insane.

One day Shanti answered their door and met a man who she recognized as the cousin of her husband. He had lived near her in the previous life. The man was there to do business with her father.

When asked, the man said he was from Muttra and had a cousin who had married a woman named Ludgi. This cousin arranged with Shanti Devi's parents to bring the husband of the deceased girl Ludgi, unannounced, to see if Shanti Devi could identify him.

No one told Shanti the identity of the visitor. When the stranger arrived, she threw her arms around him and said he was her husband. Her previous life husband and her present life parents went to the authorities with the story.

The government of India appointed a special committee of scientists to investigate Shanti's story. She was able to point out and name all of her friends and relatives from the previous life. She was able to converse with them in the dialect of Muttra, although her parents had taught her only Hindustani.

The scientists tested her by blindfolding her and getting in a carriage with her. Shanti directed the driver through the town of Muttra, where she had never been in her present life. She correctly described all the landmarks they passed. She directed them to the end of a narrow lane and said this was where she had lived. When they removed the blindfold, she could see an old man there. She identified him as her father-in-law.

Strangely, she was able to identify her two oldest children but not the youngest that she was giving birth to when she died.

That is but one of many cases of reincarnation that have

been reported. Some others are perhaps more convincing than this one. Several writers claim to have witnessed the hypnotic regression of people who remembered many previous lives.

Perhaps it would help explain some people getting information in dreams, trances and voices in their heads if you accept reincarnation as real. When a person dies, if their memory or spirit can return sometime later in another body, then they must exist in a spiritual state in between lives. There would have to be many millions of spirits at any given time to communicate with, if we could do so at will.

We have no knowledge of what the spirit state would be like. Are they constrained by time, as we in material bodies are? If spirits are not subject to time's constraints, that would explain how they could advise about future happenings.

I have read interesting speculations about how the spirit world must exist as an energy wave, such as light waves or heat waves or magnetic waves, etc. Since the brains internal communications are electrical and chemical, perhaps when a person dies, their complete memory of self can convert to an energy wave that can travel out of their body.

All religions believe in some sort of spiritual existence after death. The Hindu religion believes in reincarnation. The Christian religion believed in reincarnation before the Romans took over their religion around 300AD. The Romans revised the early Christian doctrine and deleted mention of reincarnation. They reasoned that people would more readily accept Christianity if they thought there was but one chance at salvation.

There are a number of well-documented instances of eerie and strange occurrences. One such happened to a man named David Lang.

The date was September 23, 1880. The place was David Lang's farm, a few miles from Gallatin, Tennessee. David's two children, eight-year-old George and eleven-year-old Sarah, were playing in the front yard. Mrs. Lang and David Lang came out of their house. David Lang started across a pasture in front of the house to check on his quarter horses. He had just started walking across the pasture when they spotted a horse and buggy coming up the lane towards the house. In the buggy were a friend, Judge Peck, and Judge Peck's brother-in-law.

David Lang turned in the pasture and started back towards his house to greet his friend. He had not taken a dozen steps when he disappeared, in full view of all those present.

The five observers raced across the pasture to the spot where he disappeared. There was not a tree, a bush or any sort of hole in the ground to indicate where he might have gone. The pasture was completely undisturbed. They searched all around and found nothing. By nightfall, there were scores of people on the scene and they searched the whole area, foot by foot. No trace of Lang was ever found.

The county surveyor probed the field and found it supported by a thick layer of limestone with no sinkholes or caves. David Lang was gone. He had vanished in full view of five people. One instant he was there, the next instant he was gone forever. His children said, in later years, there was a circle of stunted grass about 15 feet in diameter at the spot he disappeared.

There have been several instances of living creatures found where the laws of science dictate they could not exist.

April 22, 1881 found Joe Molino working at the sixty-foot level of the Wild West Mine near Ruby Hill, Nevada. He broke open a piece of solid rock and found a cavity filled with white worms of some sort. The worms showed no signs of life at first but soon began to move about. The worms were sent, along with the stone cavity, to the bureau of mines. A few weeks later, the bureau of mines declared that the worms could not have been found where the miners reported.

A reddish-gray beetle was found entombed in a tight fitting mold of iron ore in the Longfellow Mine near Clifton, Arizona in 1892. The beetle was given to Mr. Z. T. White, a geologist in El Paso, Texas. He placed it on a piece of paper in a specimen case. About a week after the beetle was removed from the mine, a small beetle emerged from the body of the original specimen. They placed this beetle in a jar, where it lived for several months. The ore, the beetle encased in it and the young beetle are now in the Smithsonian Institute in Washington, D.C.

At the Black Diamond coal mine near San Francisco, in 1873, miners found a large frog embedded in a limestone layer they had just blasted. The frog fitted tightly in the stone and when removed, left an exact duplicate of his shape. The frog and the surrounding limestone were brought to the surface where the frog lived for about a day, though he was blind and could only move one leg slowly. The frog and his age-old tomb are now owned by the San Francisco Academy of Sciences.

I believe this frog could have been in a state of suspended animation, which our science cannot duplicate.

The Brown and Hall Sawmill at Acton, Ontario, Canada was sawing up a large pine log in October of 1893. The workers had sawed away part of the log when they saw an unusual dark spot on the internal wood. They found a four-inch cavity, from which the head of a live toad then emerged. The cavity in which the toad was contained was nearly spherical in shape and very smooth. The tree itself was about 200 years old and that particular section was some sixty feet above ground. The toad was surrounded by solid wood nearly 30 inches thick.

The dock at George's Basin in Liverpool, England was the site of another well-documented case in 1829.

Giant blocks of granite were removed from the underwater footing of the dock. One of the blocks was cut into pieces for new steps. The cutting disclosed a small toad in a hole in the stone block. They removed it by enlarging the hole around it. The toad only lived a few hours. British scientists examined the toad and the tomb but could only shake their heads.

There are a number of mysteries involving movements of dead humans without live human help.

August twenty-fourth in 1943 on the island of Barbados a group of Masonic officials opened a sealed grave. They wished to pay tribute to Alexander Irvine whose remains were in the vault. He was the father of freemasonry on Barbados. The same vault held the remains of Sir Evan McGregor. His body was placed in the vault in 1841, after Mr. Irvine was buried there.

The vault was constructed of native stone. It extended four feet above ground, and rested on a four-foot deep brick and concrete base. Descending six steps and removing a heavy cover slab gained entrance to the bricked up doorway.

As the workmen removed the bricks, they discovered a

metal object leaning against the other side. Soon they discovered that it was a lead sheathed coffin, which they had to lower to the floor as they removed the brick. When they were able to enter the vault they discovered it was the 600-pound coffin of Sir Evan McGregor leaning, head down, against the door.

There had been no earthquakes on the island to account for the movement. Even more puzzling was the fact there was no trace of the coffin or the body of Alexander Irvine. A team of scientists were called in to investigate but were equally baffled.

There was another cemetery on Barbados, several miles away, used by the Chase family. Time after time, as members of the Chase family died and the vault reopened, the coffins were found in disarray, tumbled upside down and across the vault.

These coffins were so heavy it required eight strong men to carry them. In each case, the heavy capstone to the vault was in place, sealed with lead. There was never any sign of tampering. Only two coffins always remained unmoved. These were the coffins of Mrs. Goddard, the original occupant, and a baby girl, Mrs. Goddard's granddaughter.

Another oddity that science has yet to explain is a phenomenon called "spontaneous human combustion." There have been a number of well-documented cases of human combustion investigated, but none explained.

On Monday morning, the second day of July 1961 in St. Petersburg Florida, Mrs. P. M. Carpenter went to the door of the room occupied by Mrs. Mary H. Reeser, whom she had last seen the night before. She went because it was time for their usual morning coffee. Earlier that morning, a man trying to deliver a telegram to Mrs. Reeser had no response to his knock.

When Carpenter touched the doorknob, it was so hot it burned her hand. Some nearby housepainters helped her force open the door. Inside they found that the apartment was unbearably hot, even though the windows were open. The charred remains of a big armchair and the equally charred remains of Mrs. Reeser were near the front window.

The police, fire department and pathologist investigators all tried to determine what had happened. Mrs. Reeser's one hundred seventy pounds was reduced to less than ten pounds of charred material. Only her left foot, her shrunken skull and a few vertebrae remained. The coil springs were all that remained of the big chair. The room showed little effects of the heat. There was a sooty deposit on the walls from a point about four feet above the floor. Twelve feet from where she sat, two small candles had melted. Directly beneath the chair was a small burn mark on the rug. Beside the chair, a plastic cover of an electric wall outlet had melted. It was as if the heat that destroyed her came from within her body and had little effect outside of it.

Famed pathologist Dr. Wilton Korgman of the University of Pennsylvania also investigated Mrs. Reeser's death. His final report said, "Never have I seen a skull so shrunken nor a body so completely consumed by heat. I regard it as the most amazing thing I have ever seen."

I read a book long ago written by a man who believed in God but not in the doctrines and creeds of any of the established religions. He speculated that the earth was God's school for humans. He accepted reincarnation as true and thought each reincarnation might represent a grade in God's school. His theory proposed that we choose to reincarnate after death, exercising free will here on earth, trying to learn more from each life. Some of us make terrible mistakes and have to return repeatedly until we learn what God demands. When we have learned all we can on Earth, our spirit moves on to the next higher level. His theory is not provable but it makes as much sense as other religious superstitions.

The point I have been trying to make here is we should not be ashamed to say, "I don't know." Too many make up speculative answers to unanswerable questions because we refuse to admit, "I don't know."

We will always face questions whose answers are beyond our understanding. Learn to say, "I don't know" when faced with the unknowable. Only then can we study our world without having to deal with all the phony stories man creates to hide his ignorance.

ANCIENT TRAGEDY

I love the mountains of West Virginia where I lived the early years of my life. The mountains' unsurpassed beauty in the spring season when the wild flowers bloom is what I miss most from my youth. My present home is far from any mountains.

Twenty years ago during the spring, I decided to make a nostalgic trip to the nearest mountains to view the wild flowers. My destination was the Blue Ridge Mountains in North Carolina. I had only the weekend off work so I left soon after arriving home on Friday. I made it to the foothills of the mountains late in the evening, checked into a motel and asked for an early wake-up call.

The next morning, I drove up the nearby mountain on a secondary road until I found a wide pull-off by a mountain stream and parked there. I decided to follow the stream up the mountain valley because it would be easier walking and there would likely be more flowers growing near the water. As it happened, I found a well-worn wild animal path by the stream.

After about two hours of traveling the path by the

stream and observing the many wild flowers, I was nearing the head of the stream. The terrain had narrowed to a deep gorge with steep, near vertical cliffs of sandstone on each side. The wildflowers were plentiful in this area with many of my favorite wild flowers called Lady Slippers. The two hours of viewing the beauty of this mountain made my trip worthwhile.

During my climb, I had noticed the past winter's ice and snow had loosened many rocks which had fallen down to the stream's edge. I was about ready to end my trip and return down the mountain when I noticed a huge boulder had fallen and dammed up the stream just ahead. I decided to check out this large rock, since something about it seemed out of place.

The rock was about the size of two automobiles and had formed a pond about sixty feet long before the water had eroded a path around one edge of the stone and continued flowing. What caught my attention was the boulder had caused little disturbance to the ground where it struck. If it had fallen more than a few feet it should have made a real mess of the area where it landed, but here it had not.

The reason was obvious once I examined the cliff face just above the fallen boulder. About four feet up there was a broken ledge about four feet wide, on which the boulder had obviously rested. The part of the ledge on which it had lain had collapsed from many years of erosion. Even more interesting to note was the ledge about nine feet above this one had also collapsed sometime in the distant past and allowed the boulder to fall to its most recent precarious ledge. On the lower ledge where the stone had most recently resided, I noticed a small hole, mostly filled in with stones, which appeared to be concealing a cave.

Growing curiosity motivated me to explore this possible cave. I climbed upon the ledge and proceeded to move the small stones and gravel away to clear the entrance. When the entrance was cleared, it was unevenly shaped and approximately five feet high by three feet wide. Little light entered the cave but I could see it was much larger inside than the entrance dimensions.

The main part of the cave was about thirty feet deep and twelve feet wide. There was a small exit at the rear going deeper into the mountain. Using my cigarette lighter as a lamp, I entered the cave and checked the roof for loose stones or dangerous appearing cracks. The roof was solid and looked safe so I proceeded to explore the cave.

What I found near the right side of the cave was shocking! There lay the skeletons of three humans!

I could imagine the terrible death these people must have suffered when the boulder blocked the exit to their cave. The boulder now lying in the stream below had doomed them to a slow death from thirst and starvation. I could find no evidence of clothing or other possessions. Whatever they possessed must have been composed of organic material, which completely decomposed over the many years they were there.

Then I noticed what appeared to be the head of some kind of bird protruding from the soil near the hand of the skeleton on the right. I extinguished my lighter so I could use both hands then knelt and dug the object from the dusty soil. I stumbled from the cave into the daylight to examine what I had found.

After cleaning away the clinging dirt from the object, it appeared to be a solid chunk of wood measuring about six inches by four inches. The carved head of a bird resembling an eagle extended from one side. A closer examination revealed a thin crack completely around the wooden block near the side with the carved eagle. This led me to believe the wooden block was a small chest with the eagle's head used as the lid's handle. I used my pocketknife to pry into the exposed crack and open the lid of the chest.

What I saw inside the chest when the lid popped open amazed me. There were five beautifully shaped arrowheads, which appeared to be made of glass. I removed them, one at a time, and polished them on my shirt. When I had finished polishing the last one, I became convinced the arrowheads were not made of glass. I was sure I was holding five flawless cut diamonds in my hands.

If the arrowheads were really diamonds, however, they presented a large logistical problem. Diamonds such as these I was holding have never been found in this part of the world. Since these people were obviously from the distant past, they could not have been able to travel to places where diamonds exist. Suddenly, I remembered something odd I had vaguely noticed about the skeletons, which caused me to want a second look at them.

Again using my cigarette lighter, I reentered the cave and closely viewed the skeletons. A minute or two may have passed before the disparity of the skeletons jumped out at me. All three had only four fingers and four toes. I could believe mice or other small animals might have carried away a few bones but for all three to have the exact same bones missing was too much of a coincidence. I finally realized the three people who died here in this cave were not humans from this planet.

Now that I suspected I was looking at skeletons of beings from another world, I noticed the skulls of all three were too large to match the other bones if they had been humans. In addition, the leg and arm bones were longer and skinnier.

I am not an expert on the human anatomy, but I believed then and now, that the beings that possessed those long, thin bones came from a world with less gravity than our planet. Their large skulls probably meant they were also more intelligent than we are.

Astronomers have identified many millions of galaxies with billions of stars. The odds are overwhelming that there will be many planets around some of those stars with conditions of such that life could exist there as it does here. It is also a certainty that many of those livable planets will be much older than Earth.

Assuming we do not self-destruct our civilization, think of how advanced we might be in several thousand years. Yes, I believe I found the remains of ancient visitors from another world that day in the mountains.

I never reported my discovery to any authorities because I was afraid they would take my diamond arrowheads.

ALASKAN ADVENTURE

I was at Elmendorf AFB near Anchorage, Alaska, for three years near the end of my twenty-one year military career. Those who have been in the military forces of this country know military life can be boring except for time spent in a combat zone. This boredom often motivated me to seek out adventure when off duty. I decided to spend several days far out in the wilderness and live off the land, if I could arrange it.

A friend of mine had recently retired from the Air Force and bought a home in Anchorage. He had a small four seat aircraft equipped to land on short, unimproved dirt landing strips. I talked to him about my plan to spend a week in the Alaskan wilderness. I needed an inexpensive way to fly in and back out if I was to have my adventure. My friend offered me a good deal.

This retired Sergeant friend was in the process of building a hunting and fishing cabin by a river about one hundred and thirty miles northwest of Anchorage. This river was a branch of the Kuskokwim river. If the river branch where we were had a name, I was never told it. The

Kuskokwim is the longest river in the United States. He had a water jet powered boat already at the site and all the lumber and tools needed to build his cabin. Most of his supplies came by boat many miles from the city of Anchorage. He could reach his property by using a boat or by flying his plane there and landing on a gravel bar by the river. A tent erected near the river was for the many weekends he would need to build his cabin.

The cabin site itself was located on top of a high hill just beside the river. All supplies for building the cabin would have to be hand carried up this steep hill. My friend could use all the help he could muster.

I promised my friend I would help him build his cabin on Saturday and Sunday if he would fly me in, let me use his tent for a few days, then come back for me Wednesday. He agreed to this deal and set a time for me to meet him at the local civilian airport on Saturday morning.

Saturday morning had great flying weather and the flight into the Alaskan wilderness was uneventful. The gravel bar where we landed by the river was not really gravel. It was composed of stones, varying in size from softballs to volleyballs. His aircraft was equipped with large balloon tires designed to allow landing on rough landing strips but this rough and bumpy landing did elevate my heartbeat somewhat.

We had to carry building materials up the steep embankment from the river to the cabin site before starting the actual construction. The building project went well over the weekend and the cabin had a good start by Sunday evening.

My friend flew home Sunday evening. I was now one

hundred and thirty miles from civilization and all alone. My wilderness adventure had begun.

I had brought some dehydrated food, coffee, cooking oil, margarine and bread with me but I intended to live off the land as much as possible. The river was an angler's paradise where my dinners were still swimming. The Salmon were running and there were plenty of Cutthroat Trout and Grayling in every pool of the river. For protection from Grizzly bears, I had brought along my 30:06 caliber rifle.

Just after my coffee Monday morning, I scouted about a mile up and down the river to check what animals were my neighbors. I carried my fishing rod and some lures on my hat in case I came upon a likely looking fishing spot.

Near my camp, I found tracks of moose, beaver and black bears. The black bear's track is distinguishable from the more dangerous grizzly bear's track by the claw impressions his foot makes. Black bears can climb trees and have retractable claws. They do not leave claw impressions with their tracks. Grizzlies cannot retract their claws and you can see their impression in its paw print. The grizzly cannot climb trees but uses his extended claws for digging and killing prey.

The river had short sections of swift, white water with clear pools separating them. I could see fish in these pools between the rapids. Soon I was fishing more than I was walking.

The predominant fish was Chum Salmon, known locally as Dog Salmon. These fish were all rather large, between fifteen and twenty pounds. I had six-pound test line on my reel so the Salmon could easily break my line if I did not take a long time to tire him out before attempting to land him.

I was losing too many lures caused by the large salmon

breaking my line. I did not want to eat the salmon because they were much too large for one meal and I could not preserve the meat. Any uneaten fish lying around would attract bears.

I was careful to cast near the trout and grayling, since they were to be my main food source. I released everything I caught the first day except one dinner size grayling I wanted for lunch.

I prepared and cooked the grayling by wrapping it in aluminum foil with salt and about one inch of a stick of margarine. I placed the foil wrapped fish in the hot ashes at the edge of my campfire for about twenty minutes. I know all food tastes better in the outdoors but I swear this was the best tasting fish I had ever eaten. I ate one or two grayling or trout every day I was there.

The downriver area proved to be an angler's paradise all afternoon. Most casts resulted in me hooking a fish but I lost a few before landing. I found the same tracks of animals I had found upriver and the track of a wolf as well.

If you are wondering why I was so interested in animal tracks, I was concerned about grizzly bears in my area. Grizzlies have torn up camps looking for food and a few have attacked and killed people. I could not legally kill a grizzly bear unless he was attacking me.

The hunting season was open on black bears and I was considering killing one to make a rug of his hide. The killing of any animal I did not intend to eat bothered my conscience. I had not really decided what I would do if an opportunity to kill a black bear arose.

The next day was bear day, for sure. About one hundred yards up stream from my camp, I found tracks where a large

Grizzly had crossed the stream during the night. I was thankful the wind was blowing downriver and he did not smell my camp. I returned to camp for my rifle although it was inconvenient to carry while fishing.

Thirty minutes later, a large Black Bear came out of the riverside brush, stared at me, sniffed the air, then splashed across the stream and disappeared in the thick brush. I noticed he had rubbed a large bare spot in his fur near his front shoulder. I did not want a rug with a bare spot. I am sure the bear appreciated my perfectionism in selecting a bear rug.

During the rest of the week, I saw seven Black Bears and every one of them had rubbed bare spots in their fur. I was not tempted to shoot any of these bears.

When I tired of fishing, I explored the areas where the beaver were working. I marveled at their inefficiency. They had chewed down many trees too far from the stream to fall in the water for a dam. I am no beaver expert, so maybe they planned to come back and eat the bark later.

A light rain with fog started late Monday, which is typical Alaskan summertime weather. Tuesday evening the rain became heavier and I had to go back to camp and sit in the tent. I sat with the tent flaps open and watched the river's steady rise.

Late in the evening, I braved the rainfall long enough to catch two small grayling to eat. I had no light with me because I needed none. This far north in the middle of summer, the darkest part of the night is comparable to twilight farther south.

I awakened Wednesday morning to light rain and heavy fog cloaking the river valley. My friend was supposed to fly me home today. I doubted he could find this place with the heavy fog over the river. I listened for the sound of his airplane all day. He never came for me.

The fog and rain did not let up the next day, nor did it clear up on Friday, Saturday or Sunday. I was getting worried because I was due to return to work on Monday. I had no way of getting home. I had my friend's boat but there was not enough gas for it to travel one hundred and thirty miles to Anchorage.

Early Sunday I was looking out of the tent at the rain when I heard the sound of an airplane. The plane was coming from upriver and sounded low. Soon, it popped out of the fog and landed in front of me in the shortest landing I have ever seen. The rising river had shortened the landing strip to perhaps half its length and the plane first touched down in shallow water.

A bush pilot who was a guide for big game hunters flew the plane. He had a hunter from Texas with him. They had been high up on the mountain slopes after a trophy mountain goat. I noticed the propeller of his plane curled over about a foot on one end. I thought it was making a strange noise when it landed.

The bush pilot explained he had misjudged the upslope when landing on a glacier. The prop of his plane had dug into the ice and was bent. I explained my predicament and he suggested we could help each other.

This pilot asked me to use the jet boat to take his customer about ten miles downriver to a more improved airstrip, then return the boat to camp. He had radioed Anchorage while on the glacier and a new propeller for his plane was on its way there now. The same plane would take his customer back to Anchorage. When I returned with the boat, we would take the risk of flying his damaged plane to the little field ten miles downstream where the new prop would arrive.

The boat trip with the Texan was rather exciting during the whitewater stretches of river but I made it down and back with little trouble. I had maybe a cup of gas left in the boat's outboard engine when I returned.

I loaded my few things in his plane and he taxied upstream on the gravel bar until his large balloon tires were nearly covered with water. Just at the other end of the gravel bar, the river made a turn to the right. Directly across the river in line with our flight path was a line of rather tall trees. When my friend flew out last Sunday evening, he had to make a sharp bank to the right as soon as he lifted off to avoid the trees.

My bush pilot revved his engine to maximum and we started to move slowly down the gravel bar. Our rate of acceleration was so low I felt sure we could not lift off by the turn in the river.

We did, but just barely. We were too low to bank to the right so he climbed as fast as the bent prop would allow, headed straight for the trees across the river. I felt sure we would crash right there. The wheels of his plane tore through the top branches of the trees. We only had a small loss of altitude then continued down river. My bush pilot laughed and thought our narrow escape was funny. I had trouble laughing with him.

We landed the plane ten miles down the river without incident. His Texan customer had departed for Anchorage and the new propeller was there. We installed the new propeller in short order and took off for home.

I learned more about a bush pilot's life on the flight back to Anchorage. This guide offered his customers a package deal on the five Alaskan big game trophies. These were the grizzly bear, black bear, moose, mountain goat and dall sheep. His recent customer from Texas had killed one of each, except the mountain goat. He had damaged his plane on the glacier looking for a trophy goat.

This guide was telling me how he often flew a customer to an area where they would spot the animal they wanted. Alaskan law required he land the plane and let the customer out. The customer must wait until the next day before he could legally shoot any animal after flying to it. Most guides and hunters ignored the law, he claimed. He did not directly admit doing this himself.

He pointed to a small lake ahead and said he had often had customers find trophy moose at lakes like the one below. He suddenly put the plane into a steep dive and only pulled up when we were just a few feet over the lake waters. Sure enough, several Moose were feeding there and ran splashing for cover.

I called my wife from the airport in Anchorage and asked her to come take me home. She was a very worried lady who was delighted to hear from me. She had been calling everyone trying to locate me.

My friend in Anchorage, who was supposed to return for me Wednesday, apologized for not flying out to get me. He was not experienced enough as a bush pilot to land under the rainy, foggy conditions the water shortened runway.

I told him, "All's well that ends well."

LUCKY SISTER-IN-LAW

I installed and serviced burglar alarms for banks and commercial business establishments at one time. The work required me to work sometimes in police dispatch offices where the alarms terminated. Many police dispatch offices are in the county jail building, where I met some prisoners.

Most police departments use prisoners, called trustees, to do the cleaning and some other jobs around the jail building. While awaiting the telephone company to repair defective burglar alarm lines, I have had many interesting conversations with these trustees. I would like to tell you of one such conversation which may be of interest to you. I believe you and your husband were the ones about which this prisoner was talking.

This happened more than twenty years ago when I went to a neighboring county jail to repair the burglar alarm of a bank. The alarm terminals were located at one end of the building in the police dispatch office. The rest of the building was the jail. I quickly determined the problem was with the phone lines and reported it to the phone company. I waited there for the phone repairman to check the line and call me.

There was a pay phone in the hallway near the dispatcher with a bench nearby, so there is where I waited.

I observed a trustee mopping the long hallway in which I sat. When he completed the job, he came and sat beside me on the bench and asked for a cigarette. The bench on which we sat was a designated smoking area for the jail with an ashtray so I gave him a cigarette. We had a conversation while he smoked that may be of interest to you, sister-in-law.

The trustee prisoner said his name was William but everyone called him Willy. Willy was a white man and about five feet, ten inches in height. My best estimate of his age would be the mid thirties. Willy seemed happier than other prisoners did so I asked him how he could be so happy while in jail. He told me, "I was just told this morning I will be released tomorrow on parole. I have been smiling ever since." Willy had appeared before the parole board that morning.

I asked, "How long have you been in jail?"

"I received a six months sentence for cocaine possession and have served two and one-half months," Willy said, laughing. "If the judge had known everything I did while sniffing coke, I would never get out of jail."

Willie explained, "I was the main cocaine supplier for the upper part of this state for several years. A mafia type gangster came there and threatened to kill me. I knew it was time to get out of town, so I moved to the lower part of this state, where I had friends. The cops finally caught me with dope and arrested me. Fortunately, I had only a small amount of cocaine in my possession. I was not charged with selling dope, only possession."

Willy vowed, "I will never sell any dope again. I don't think I have the aptitude to be a big time dope dealer."

Smiling he said, "I even tried to kill two people one time. Despite my best efforts, they are still walking around somewhere. I always thought killing people would be easy if I decided to do it."

"What was your problem?" I asked. Willy then told me a story that I think had you and your husband as co-stars.

Willie began, "I had the phone number of a Columbian in Miami, Florida. Whenever I needed more cocaine to sell, I would call the Columbian, settle on the amount and the price and agree on a meeting place both of us thought safe. This time we agreed to meet in a particular campground in North Carolina on a Saturday. We expected the campground would be so busy on a Saturday that no one would pay us any attention.

"I arrived at the campground Saturday morning and set up my camper in the spot I had reserved. I did not expect the deliveryman from Florida until late in the evening. While waiting, I wandered around the campground checking out everyone, and especially those parked nearest to me.

"I talked to the couple in the camper nearest to me. They were friendly folks and did not arouse any suspicion they might rip me off or be undercover cops. The man's name stuck in my mind because he introduced himself as "Pinky," which I think is an unusual name for a man.

"The deliveryman was not due until ten that evening and I became nervous because of the large amount of cash locked in my camper. Therefore, I started snorting my stash of coke. It gave me the courage I wanted while lowering my caution, which I needed more. When the deliveryman arrived at ten that evening, I was sure I was the most brilliant dope dealer in the country.

"The cash for dope exchange went off without a hitch. The deliveryman was the same I had used several times previously so we were on friendly terms. We snorted a line of coke together and swapped dope dealing stories for about an hour.

"My dope delivery guy then left for Florida. I did not want to attract any curiosity by leaving in the middle of the night. I decided to wait until the next day to leave the campground.

"The next morning my mind was clear from the cocaine effects and I began removing the camper hook-ups in preparation to leave.

"The first bad feeling happened when I saw my camper window nearest where me and the deliveryman had been talking was open. The second "Oh, no!" was when I noticed the nearest neighbor, Pinky, had his window open too close to mine for comfort.

"The campground was noisier this morning than last night but when I paused near their open window, I could hear Pinky and his wife clearly. She was saying, "I am going to call and let them know.

"That was all I needed to hear to confirm my suspicion that I was overheard last night talking to the deliveryman. I decided to eliminate these two campers.

"I do not like guns and had never fired one. I kept a snub-nosed revolver equipped with a silencer in my camper only because I felt any self respecting dope dealer ought to have one. What I did not know at the time was all snub nosed pistols are notorious for being inaccurate beyond ten feet. If a silencer is used it will decrease the accuracy even more.

'However, I was convinced this man Pinky and his wife

must be killed before they talked to the police. I felt the cops would surely arrest me if they learned of my conversation last night.

"I removed my pistol from the briefcase where I kept the newly purchased cocaine. From inside my camper I could see Pinky's wife as she began walking from her camper towards the campground pay phones. Concealing the pistol under my shirt, I hurried behind a row of campers to beat her there.

"The nearest place of concealment to the pay phones was about fifty feet away behind bushes. There is where I hid and waited. I watched her approach the phones and planned to wait until she stopped and started to dial the phone. Then I would shoot her like a sitting duck, so to speak. I could then go to their camper and finish off her husband, Pinky.

"All the movies I had seen made killing someone seem simple. Just point the gun at your victim, pull the trigger and they immediately fall down dead. Imagine my surprise when I pointed my pistol at this woman, pulled the trigger, and the gun made a muffled "phut" sound -- and she continued to dial the phone. Absolutely nothing happened to her.

"What I lacked in skill with the pistol I made up for with determination. The second shot did have visible results when a small twig fell from the tree by the pay phones. The lady calmly watched it fall while she continued with her phone conversation. The third shot had the most dramatic results when a bird fell from a tree on the other side of her. She continued her conversation, totally unaware of any danger.

"I was becoming very frustrated. I rapidly fired the last three bullets in my pistol thinking one must kill her. I had no such luck. She finished her phone call and, smiling all the way, walked back to her camper.

"Getting out of the campground before the arrival of the cops was now my highest priority. As I drove my camper quickly away, I saw no sign of Pinky or his wife. I felt sure they were watching my every move and had a suspicion she was writing down my license number.

"While I drove away, I suddenly realized if I could somehow eliminate Pinky, and his wife, there would be no witnesses to appear against me in court. Therefore, I went only a short way down the highway and hid my camper on a dirt side road. The spot I parked allowed me a view of the campground entrance.

"Only a few minutes passed before my fears were confirmed. A deputy sheriff's car entered the campground, stayed just a few minutes then sped off down the highway past where I was hid. I was sure they were searching for my camper.

"Realizing I was in deep trouble, I snorted two lines of coke while trying to plan my next move. I had no more bullets for my pistol and doubted I could kill anything with it anyway. Then I remembered something Pinky said during the previous day's conversation. He said they were going home Sunday about noon, which was about now.

"Looking across the highway from where I was concealed, I could see a deep gulch. I felt sure it would be fatal for the occupants of any camper forced off the road at this point. There was no guardrail along the road to hinder my plan.

"If I could time it just right and come charging out of the side road just as they drove past, I could bump them over the edge. While I was thinking about it, I saw their camper leave the campground and start down the highway towards me.

"As he started my camper, I noticed one drawback to my plan. The trees would hide my view of their camper until they were almost right in front of me. On second thought, the trees should be no problem. I was so high and alert on dope, it would be no problem to estimate their camper's speed and come charging out at just the right moment.

"Well, it was not my day. I came roaring out of the side road and saw their camper flash by before I reached the intersection. Unfortunately, I could not stop in time and went over the edge into the deep gulch.

"I awakened in a nearby hospital. I had a bad concussion but no other serious injuries. A deputy sheriff came to the hospital and questioned me. He only asked me how the accident happened. I realized then that I had misinterpreted the whole situation.

"I was lucky in more ways than one. The police had my vehicle towed to the nearest junkyard and never found my briefcase filled with cocaine. I stayed in the dope business there for a while longer until the bad people arrived in town. '

"I believe the couple you tried to kill was my sister-in-law and her husband. He is the only man I ever knew named Pinky," I said.

Willy begged me to apologize for him. He said, "If you tell them the story of what happened, even though they were unaware of anything happening, they might forgive me."

I never heard from Willie again but national statistics indicate he probably returned to using and selling dope.

Please remember Willy, sister-in-law, and keep your camper's windows closed in the future.

GUARDIAN ANGELS

Tigers are adaptable animals and some still live in the wild in Asia. They range from the tropics to Siberia. There are many myths and legends about this animal in Asia. Despite intense pressure from human overpopulation in China and India, a few Tigers remain wild and free.

These large cats sometimes reach nine feet in length. They are natural predators and have killed and eaten humans when other prey was not available.

I believe Tigers are the most beautiful and graceful of the large cats. The potential threat they pose just adds to their mystique. All around the world, Zoos have Tigers on display. When you observe one up close, they have a special aura, even in a Zoo.

My Grandson, I will now tell you about a Tiger who once visited me. An animal I met was perhaps more than a Tiger. I will let you decide if this was my hallucination or actually happened.

I rolled in my wheelchair to my back patio to enjoy the first cool afternoon of the fall season. I like to observe the birds and squirrels at the birdfeeder in my back yard when the weather permits. My little black dog was asleep beside me and I was very relaxed. As sometimes happens when I am alone and have no distractions, my mind drifted down strange paths. I began thinking about Guardian Angels.

I pondered how some people, whether through bad luck or bad choices, seem constantly on the edge of disaster. Some can nimbly sidestep, skip and jump on the edge and always avoid major trouble. Others seem to wind up in deep trouble every time they approach any difficulty. I have several acquaintances of both types.

I was wondering what could account for the difference in outcome when both types faced essentially the same problems. I was tempted to think the difference is the strength of their characters but the incidents I have observed disputes that conclusion. I have known some good people who suffered one disaster after another while many low-life people avoided trouble. I speculated, for lack of a better answer, that some people might have Guardian Angels while others do not.

Just at this point in my ruminations, I noticed a movement at the edge of the forest behind my house. A large animal walked out from the trees and made a long, graceful leap over the drainage ditch behind my fenced yard. I watched as it made another effortless leap over my fence and into my yard. I recognized the animal as a beautiful, fully-grown Bengal Tiger.

To say I was frightened would be a gross understatement; I was terrified. I understood immediately I was at the Tiger's mercy. He could attack me long before I could propel my wheelchair back inside my house. However, even with my fear, I noticed something was definitely disharmonious about what I was observing.

The Tiger stood about ten feet from my birdfeeder. The birds and two squirrels continued to feed there. My dog awakened and looked around the yard, then lay back down, undisturbed by a threat I could plainly see.

I suspected I was dreaming or hallucinating. A Tiger escaping from a Carnival or Fair in the area would have been on the local news, but was not. This large beast had slinked across the lawn and sat directly before me as I sat at the edge of my patio.

The Tiger and I stared into each other's eyes. I was relieved to notice his body language did not suggest I was to be his prey. He did not have the twitching tail and wide mouth snarl, which would indicate he was about to pounce on me. Instead, his gaze seemed to focus distantly. Then this huge cat said, "I overheard your thoughts and have come to tell you about Guardian Angels."

I have always considered myself a sane, stable, down to earth type man. You can imagine my shock at what I was seeing and hearing right before me. I was amazed at how everything around me seemed completely normal except for this Tiger. This did not feel like a dream. I decided to go along with this crazy Tiger vision in hopes of learning more.

I asked the Tiger "Are you my Guardian Angel?"

"I am a Guardian Angel, but not yours," he replied.

"Will you explain to me who you really are and why you are here?" I asked the Tiger.

"I am assigned to your Grandson and all his family as their Guardian Angel. I need you to explain some things to them so I can be more effective.

"You see, everyone has a Guardian Angel but some have

not learned how to listen to their advice. Before each decision a person makes or action he takes in life, there comes a moment when he can hear the advice of his Guardian Angel. They must make a conscious pause and ask themselves, "Is this the right thing to do?" Many people call it listening to their conscience. If they do not ask for and listen to the advice, they often make bad decisions and get into trouble.

"Perhaps it would be useful to tell your Grandson, his wife, and two children just what a Guardian Angel represents. All Guardian Angels are the immortal spirits of departed ancestors of the family they try to advise. They want to help because of the love they have for the living. Usually their advice is in the form of the person's conscience. On rare occasions, Guardian Angels will take a physical form to help the family members in need.

"Guardian Angels can also be useful in other ways. When devastated with grief after losing a loved one, the spiritual ancestors add their strength to yours and give you relief from sorrow.

"Your spiritual ancestor's strength may also be given to those who feel hopeless and lost because of problems riding too heavily on their shoulders. If the troubled will only open their minds to the strength of their spiritual family, they will be better able to persevere through all life's problems.

"A Guardian Angel cannot take any physical action to help you. He can only influence your thinking. A Guardian Angel cannot do other things such as shield you from all the hurts and worries of life. He can only give strength and advice to avoid some problems and survive the rest with your smile intact.

"Remember, family spirits who love you note everything

you do or say. They want only the best for you from life's great opportunity to learn from living. Keep in mind that you will join the spiritual world someday. Live so you will be remembered on earth for the number of people who loved and respected you and not for any material wealth you accumulated.

The Tiger stood as if to depart so I asked, "Why do you think my grandson will listen to me if he ignores your attempts to advise him?"

The Tiger was smiling when he replied, "Because he is unaware of my existence. He never leaves a mental opening for me to advise him. I hope he will believe I really exist after you tell him about our talk today."

"Before you leave, please answer one more question for me. Why do you appear before me as a Tiger? I asked.

"Because I felt a fierce Tiger image would grab your attention more so than, say, a bunny rabbit. Was I successful with my appearance?" he asked.

The Tiger then turned and made just a few leaps before disappearing into the trees behind my house. My dog and the birds and squirrels were not disturbed.

My beloved Grandson, I hope you will always listen to your conscience. Whenever you see a Tiger or a picture of one, remember your Guardian Angel and listen to his advice.

HYPNOTIZED SISTER

The more science learns about our consciousness, the more mysterious it becomes. Hypnosis is a good example of our mind's strangeness. A Frenchman named Mesmer first discovered hypnotism and the practice was called Mesmerism for many years.

Hypnotists have entertained crowds with their skills. You may have seen hypnotists on television or stage shows. To amuse an audience, he might tell a hypnotized subject he is a baby and have him nurse a bottle or cry, just as a baby would. The entertainment aspect of hypnotism is subject to fraud and deception. We cannot know how much we see on the television or stage is true hypnotism.

Doctors have used hypnotism to control pain. Therapists have used it to change harmful behavior patterns of their patients. Law enforcement has used hypnotism to improve the recall of witnesses. These uses of hypnotism are not always successful but the success rate is sufficiently high for it to be worthwhile to try when other methods have failed.

The accuracy of the information gained from a person

under hypnosis is controversial. Many believe the hypnotist can suggest something and the subject will relate it as a factual experience. The courts of this country do not accept information gained from hypnosis. The cases of UFO abductions reported by persons under hypnosis have cast doubt on hypnosis' reliability. The same is true of people reporting previous lives while hypnotized.

The early users of hypnotism believed a subject under hypnotism would not do anything they would not do when not in a hypnotic state. This has proven to be untrue in recent years. Highly skilled hypnotists can have a subject do almost anything if they first tell the subject he is in a situation where the action the hypnotist is asking for is a normal thing to do. For example, a hypnotist might tell a subject he is locked in his bathroom preparing to take a bath, and then tell him to remove all his clothing. The subject would comply because, in this context, it was the normal thing to do.

My sister, I want to tell you about a hypnotist I met in a bar many years ago and some of the strange things he told me. I hope it will not be distressing to you. This man seemed to know you quite well.

A rainy Saturday in late October of 1963 was when it happened. The sky was overcast and producing a drizzle of rain when I arose in the morning and continued to be dark and dreary on through the afternoon. A recent frost had caused the last of the leaves to fall from the trees. Just to look at the bare forest on the mountainsides on this dark day was depressing.

Having canceled my plan to hunt Pheasant that day, I could think of nothing else to do but find a warm bar and drink as much beer as my belly would hold. I have to admit drinking beer was a favorite activity of mine back then.

I was a twenty-four years old member of the U. S. Air force and had just returned from a one-year tour of duty in South Korea. The Air Force gave me thirty days leave before shipping me to Germany for three years.

I usually enjoyed my rare visits home but this one was not going too well. Many of my old acquaintances there had moved away and those few left were busy with their families and jobs. Consequently, I was alone much of this leave and I needed something to occupy my time.

I borrowed a family member's car and started bar hopping at a bar near home at mid-afternoon. I proceeded to go to the next bar up the highway after one beer at each bar. By eight in the evening, I had arrived at the last bar I intended to visit before going home. I had not found any irresistible women or anything else of interest, except cold beer. The last bar I visited that dreary night had a large crowd of drinkers. I sat on one of the last empty barstools.

My attention was drawn to a booth in a back corner where a large, loud group of guys and gals were having a good time. All of their attention was on a man in his mid to late thirties who they called "Wiz" or "Wizard."

We all watched quietly as he began to swing a round medallion on a gold chain in front of the face of one of the young men seated there. He was talking quietly to the young man as he sat across from him in the booth. In just a few minutes, he put the medallion down and told the young man there was a wastebasket in the middle of the dance floor and asked if he saw it. The young man said he did see the wastebasket. Of course, there was no wastebasket there.

"Please empty our ashtray into the wastebasket," the Wiz

said. The young fellow immediately got up and emptied the ashtray in the middle of the dance floor, returned and sat back down in the booth. Everyone was laughing except the waitress cleaning up the mess when the young man came out of his hypnotic trance.

Wiz did not attempt to hypnotize anyone else and soon the crowd began to thin out. When all his friends had left, he came to the bar and sat two stools down from me. I noticed he walked as if he was more than half-drunk. He spoke to me and seemed a friendly drunk so we started a conversation.

I asked if he had really hypnotized the young man or if they had it planned beforehand. He claimed he was a real hypnotist and had learned to hypnotize from his Uncle while a teenager. His Uncle was a hypnotist who traveled with a carnival but spent his winters with his family. He then asked my name.

When I told him my name, I saw his face light up and he asked if I knew a woman named Joyce with the same last name. He ordered us both a beer when I told him you were my sister. The Wizard looked at me with a sad expression and said; "I have loved your sister since she was twelve years old."

Anyone familiar with drunks will know they tend to exaggerate, and often lie while under the influence of alcohol. I considered this as he talked about you, but he was a convincing storyteller.

Wizard did not tell me how he first met you but said, "I schemed and contrived to be near Joyce at every opportunity when we went to school together. She flirted with many young men but treated me like a brother. Until she married, I was sure she would someday see me and return the love I felt for her."

I am not easy to anger but what he told me next still upsets me when I think of it.

The Wizard continued, "I was driving back from work one evening when I saw Joyce walking beside the highway near her home. I stopped to talk with her and parked near the school bus stop by the roadside. Joyce told me she was going to visit a friend who lived just a little further down the road.

"I loved her so much but she showed no interest in me. This inspired me to hypnotize her. She did not know I was capable of hypnotizing anyone so I was able to accomplish it without her becoming aware of what was occurring. I gave her a post-hypnotic order to forget the whole incident so she would never know what happened that night."

The Wiz did not go into detail about all that happened while you were hypnotized. He began to cry after he said, "The only time I ever kissed her was that night."

He paid the bartender for his tab then and said, "I know I am getting too drunk. I better go home now."

I followed him outside to his car and wanted to kick his butt but there were too many people around. In his drunken state, he remained completely unaware his story had upset me.

"I want to show you something," the Wiz said and he opened the trunk of his car.

Removing a small box from the trunk of his car, he held it up for me to see. He opened the box and it was full of jewelry that looked expensive to me, although I am no expert on such things.

"I bought this jewelry as birthday gifts for Joyce over many years until I finally gave up hope of her ever leaving her husband," he said. The Wiz then drove away.

I waited a few minutes before I got in my car and followed him. Perhaps the Wiz was not the only one drinking too much that night. I was wondering what, if anything, I should do to a man who may have molested my sister.

Going to the law at this late date would be of no help. If what the Wiz told was all true, you would not remember the incident and I could prove nothing. I also knew, because he was so drunk, the next day he would not recall our conversation. Another complication, I was leaving for Germany in three days.

I decided justice would be served if I deprived him of his jewelry, which reminded him so much of you.

Turning off my headlights, I continued to follow the Wizard's weaving car after he turned onto a dirt lane that led to a house two miles out of the town. After parking, he staggered into the dark house and turned on lights so I guessed he must live there alone. I parked right behind him. I expected he would pass out soon from the alcohol he had consumed. I waited maybe twenty minutes before I got out of my car.

I knew there was a toolbox in the trunk of the car I was driving. I found a pry-bar in it that I used to open his car's trunk. In just a matter of a few minutes, I had all his jewelry and was on my way home.

The jewelry rightly belongs to you, since the Wizard bought it for you. I probably should have given you the jewelry back then but I could not bring myself to tell you where it came from and how I came to have it.

Unfortunately, I was short of money several times during the years since, so I sold all the jewelry.

TALKING CATBIRD

Most of us sometimes use analogies to be better understood or to make a point. We tend to anthropomorphize most animals and use many of them to construct analogies. To anthropomorphize is to attribute human characteristics to an animal that he does not have. Some examples of this are:
- Drinks like a fish
- Hungry as a bear
- Eats like a pig
- Eats like a bird
- Mean as a snake
- Sitting in the catbird's seat

These analogies do have a connection to certain characteristics of the animal named. Some analogies still in common use are ancient and the relationship between the meaning and any attribute of the animal is difficult to identify.

An example of a vague analogy is "Sitting in the Catbirds seat." Its modern meaning is to be in control or to have an advantage. I have no idea how this relates to the actual bird.

The catbird's habitat stretches from South Carolina north into Canada and west to the Great Lakes region. They are slate gray songbirds and make a mewing sound similar to a cat. Catbirds will sometimes make sounds imitating other birds, birdcalls similar to what the much better known mocking bird does.

I have observed Catbirds many times and have not seen any behavior pattern suggesting they have an advantage over other birds. Perhaps we would need to live closer to nature and observe these birds, as did the early pioneers of this country, before we could understand this term they originated.

My beloved Granddaughter, you do not need to understand the origin of the expression, "Sitting in the Catbird's seat," to appreciate the story I want to tell you now.

This incident happened to me in November of the year 1978 on a cloudy and dim Saturday afternoon with intermittent light rain. In spite of the bad weather, I became obsessed with an urge to go hunting. My obsession always happens in the fall of the year when the leaves start falling.

My yearly trips to the forests and fields are not motivated by a blood lust for game animals. I never killed any animal I did not want to eat, except snakes and rats. I did not shoot anything on many of my hunting trips. Observing the wildlife in their beautiful surroundings and the bright fall colors of the leaves gave me pleasure.

Most years South Carolina's low country woodlands are not nearly as colorful during the fall season as the mountains. Occasionally, however, we will have the colorful leafs here, as bright and beautiful as anything the mountains have to offer.

I have learned that the night temperatures must drop below freezing before the tree's sap retreats to its roots in order to have the beautiful colors. This must have happened that year because the brilliant, multi-colored foliage was truly breathtaking.

There are no lazy animals in the fall of each year. Mother Nature drives each of them at a breakneck pace to prepare for the approaching winter. I enjoy walking deep into the forest, finding a seat on a fallen tree log and observing the frantic activity all around me. Spending an afternoon doing this in autumn's splendor has often served to restore my perspective and preserve my sanity.

I drove to the Francis Marion National Forest on a Saturday afternoon. I was determined to enjoy my visit to the forest in spite of the continuing rain drizzle. Scouting for a likely place to find animals, I drove most of the dirt roads of the National Forest, which were accessible to vehicles.

I selected a spot new to me, parked my auto and walked into the forest. A fifteen-minute walk brought me to a grove of huge Live Oak trees interspersed with a few Red Oak and Hickory trees. Finding a large log for a seat, I sat and watched nature's glory in the dim light of that drizzly day.

Granddaughter, you were living with your Grandmother and me at the time. You worked near our home five days each week. What made me nervous was you drove about 125 miles each weekend to visit with your friends in the town where your parents raised you. I was very concerned for your safety. You usually made these trips after dark on Friday and Sunday nights. I knew you were at the age when young people feel they are immortal. You thought speed limits were just amusing restrictions for others to obey. Your attitude about driving did nothing to decrease my anxiety.

I felt responsible for your safety and worried each weekend until you arrived home on Sunday night. This concern for your safety was the only sandpaper to scratch my serenity as I sat on the log in the Francis Marion National Forest that wet fall day.

Many Squirrels were about feeding on the small acorns of the Live Oak trees. They had competition for the nuts from many blue jays and black birds. The nut shells fell like the rain as the squirrels and birds fed as though in a race to strip the trees of their nuts.

I studied my surroundings and noticed the remains of a long ago collapsed house among the trees. All that remained were the stones from the foundation and several fallen chimneys. The large area covered by the foundation indicated it might have been a large plantation house in the distant past.

My observation of the plantation house ruins was suddenly interrupted by what sounded like a cat mewing. The sound was coming from a large cluster of bushes that may have been lawn shrubbery at one time. I suspected someone's housecat had become lost in these woods.

I stood and walked towards the bushes until I could see the source of the sound. The mewing came from a gray bird, which seemed to be distressed. This bird was hopping from branch to branch and making the mewing sound continuously. I recognized it as a catbird because of the sound it made.

Walking around the bush, I discovered why it was so upset. This catbird had a nest in the bush and just below it was a large blacksnake. I knew blacksnakes could climb trees and feed on bird's eggs or newly hatched birds. I decided to watch this little drama play out to its natural conclusion and not interfere. Eerie things begin to happen then.

The catbird fluttered to a branch near me and said, "Well shoot the nasty thing. What are you waiting for?"

You had better believe the talking bird raised the hair on the back of my neck and quickened my heartbeat. I was sure there were no catbird's that could speak in any language beside birdcalls. I decided this must be some sort of dream or hallucination. "Did you speak to me?" I asked.

"I certainly did. Are you just going to stand there and let the snake eat this bird's babies?" She spoke with the voice of an old woman.

I decided to help this talking catbird. I placed my shotgun safety in the off position then shot the blacksnake's head off. The snake fell to the ground beneath the bush.

There was a sudden rush of many bird's wings as they all took flight. The squirrels ran and hid. The forest was suddenly as quiet as a tomb. I could hear only the quiet sound of the rain dripping from the trees. The catbird still sat on the branch just in front of me.

I looked the catbird in the eye and said, "I cannot believe I am standing here talking with a bird."

She laughed and then gave me an explanation. She said, "I am the spirit of the woman who lived my whole life in the plantation house once standing here. Having once run the plantation and all its slaves, I still take an interest in it. I often use the bodies of birds to travel around the place.

"Being a ghost on my old plantation is the penance I must pay for owning slaves and all the other misdeeds of my life. A long time must still pass before my spirit can leave this old plantation area and go to a better spiritual place."

I wanted to leave then since talking to a Catbird, which was really a ghost, was making me nervous.

She hopped to a limb closer to me and said, "I want to reward you for helping my catbird friend. It is beyond my capabilities to give you any material thing but I can tell you a little of the future to ease your worries. You can stop worrying about your Granddaughter on her weekend drives. Death or injury in an auto accident will not be her fate. Her abundance of common sense and her high energy level will see her through the difficult times of her life.

"Your Granddaughter will soon marry and give birth to a baby daughter. This great-granddaughter will grow to be a strong person and make all her family proud of her accomplishments. She will be sitting in the catbird's seat."

I left for home that day thinking I must have dozed off and all I remembered happening was but a dream. However, a strange thing happened when I visited the same place the next year. Well, that is another story for another time.

I do not ask you and your daughter to believe this story. Feel free to believe I dozed off on that log and dreamed the whole thing. Dark and drizzly afternoons may cause weird dreams if one falls into a light sleep. Perhaps this story is the result of just such a dream. However, it seemed real to me then while it was happening and was still believable when I returned home.

If you wish, I can give you directions to that special place in the forest so you can go there some dark day and question the old woman yourself.

MOTHER NATURE'S DESIRES

A new schoolteacher named Mr. Gowers and his mother moved into our neighborhood in 1954. My brother, three years older than me, became acquainted with Mr. Gowers at our High School where Mr. Gowers taught some classes. I was only thirteen years old at the time and never became acquainted with Mr. Gowers or his Mother.

As I recall, my brother and various other of Mr. Gowers' students visited him at his home quite often. His Mother was of particular interest to them because she claimed to communicate with the spiritual world. This group of Mr. Gower's students participated in some of her sessions with the Ouija board

I became more interested when my brother claimed Mrs. Gowers had taught him a chant. This chant supposedly could call up the earth spirit known as Mother Nature. Mrs. Gowers believed Mother Nature existed in both spiritual and material form.

Naturally, I begged my brother to teach me the chant, but he refused. He said Mrs. Gowers had told him he must be alone and in a remote area for the chant to work properly. My brother said he intended to try the chant the next Saturday. I resolved to track him like a bloodhound and learn his secret chant.

Mom kept us busy with various chores around the house that next Saturday until early afternoon. I rushed through my chores so I would be able to follow my brother. I pretended supreme disinterest in his activities but watched out the window when he finally left the house. I observed the direction he was going and became almost certain of his destination.

If there is any such thing as a spiritual place for me, and I think for my brother as well, it would be our family cemetery and the forested area around it. This cemetery contains the remains of many of our ancestors. The tombstones and the thick tree growth surrounding the cemetery seemed to possess a supernatural aura and gave me a sense of its otherworldliness. My brother and I often went past it on our way hunting but never hunted near the graves and never discussed why we did not. I felt sure he had chosen this place to perform the Mother Nature chant.

There were two ways to reach our cemetery from home. I watched to see which my brother went, and then I chose to go the other way. I arrived first because I ran all the way.

My first priority was to find a place of concealment commanding a view of the area. My choice was a thick patch of mountain laurel situated near the cemetery. I crawled into the center of the laurel patch and scraped away the dry leaves and twigs so I could remain silent while in hiding. Almost immediately, I heard my brother's footsteps in the leaves and saw him approaching.

An ancient downed beech tree trunk lay across the path

about twenty feet from where I was hiding. My brother climbed over this tree trunk, then turned and viewed the woodlands all around him. He sat down after assuring he was alone. As I observed him, I could see many tombstones in the background about thirty yards away.

My brother sat there for a few minutes doing nothing, but perhaps contemplating whether he really wanted to do the chant.

Then he clasped his hands to his chest in a praying gesture and began to mumble the chant. If he had given the chant in a normal tone of voice, I was near enough to have heard his words; but no, he had to mumble. Brother chanted three times with perhaps a short pause between chants.

About five feet in front of where he sat was a large standing beech tree beside the path. I did not hear or see any sign of her but suddenly she was there. Mother Nature was standing in the path directly before him and near the large beech tree.

I almost wet my pants. She was at least six feet tall, had very tan skin and was naked as a jaybird. I had never seen a woman so well endowed, or so much of any woman. I suspect my brother had not either.

She stepped forward and stood just before him with her big boobs about six inches from his face. In a high pitched and feminine voice she said, "Who calls me from my work?"

I could tell from my brother's body language that he was terrified. He said, "I didn't mean to bother you. I did not know the chant would bring you here. I was expecting something like a ghost. Who are you?"

She then smiled and said, "You may call me Mother Nature. I am responsible for all living things here on this earth. I struggle to keep everything in balance." She then sat beside him on the log.

I do not recall all he and Mother Nature discussed but mostly, he listened as she talked. She said, "I should be angry with you for disturbing me for a frivolous reason but since you are such a nice looking young man, I will talk with you a few minutes."

Much of her conversation was bitching about her problems. She complained, "The human species is becoming more of a problem. I have great difficulty trying to keep people in balance with the rest of nature. Disease and severe climatic conditions have previously sufficed to keep your numbers in balance, just as with other living things, but your species' growing technology in medicine and agriculture is subverting my plans.

"If mankind does not soon recognize the problem and reduce his numbers of his own volition, I must create massive upheavals beyond your control to reinstate the balance I require."

Mother Nature then arose and said, "I must get back to work soon but before I go, I am going to take advantage of this opportunity and you must help me." She then pulled my brother down behind the log and out of my view. For the next fifteen minutes, I could see nothing. I was afraid she was doing my brother harm but was too terrified to approach and give assistance.

When they both finally stood again, my brother was trembling from head to toe. He jumped over the downed beech tree and ran off in the direction of home.

Mother Nature either stepped behind or into the large standing Beech tree and was no longer visible. I never saw her again. When I arrived home, Mom said, "Your brother must be ill with a cold. He came in the house and went straight to bed."

I did not talk to my brother until a week later. I did not know how to bring the subject up. Finally, I asked, "Did you ever get to perform the chant Mrs. Gowers taught you?"

He said, "What chant? She never taught me a chant. You must be dreaming." I was never able to get him to acknowledge anything happened.

Secretly, I have always envied my brother's tryst with Mother Nature.

BUTTERNUT TREES OR ROSES

I lived in rural West Virginia for the first eighteen years of my life and became familiar with the natural world and the plants and animals there. My father and grandfather both taught me to recognize many of the local plant and animal species. They also taught me which were useful and which could be harmful. I want to tell you a story of some strange events involving a tree with edible nuts called a Butternut tree.

My best friend during my teen years lived on a farm about one-half mile from my home. We used a path through the intervening woodlands as a shortcut when we visited.

There was a large butternut tree near our pathway. I often noticed one of the workhorses belonging to my friend's father was standing under this tree when it was not working in the fields. Other horses and cows were in the pasture but only this one brown horse stood under this butternut tree.

Our curiosity was aroused so one day my friend and I went under the tree to see what was attracting the horse. We had a strange, mind-bending experience there. It was thirty minutes before we walked away from the tree and talked of how we were affected.

We became very relaxed as soon as we walked under the

tree. Everything looked normal with leaves and old butternut shells on the ground. We saw nothing that might attract a horse.

We became so relaxed; we sat on the ground for thirty minutes. My friend and I were very active boys. For us to sit for thirty minutes was totally out of character and contrary to what our normal activity was.

What we were thinking during these thirty minutes was the strangest thing. My thoughts were like a complete summary of my life, from my first memory to the present. My friend reported he had the exact same experience. We did not like the eerie feeling this gave us, so we left that area and did not return for almost a week.

We discussed what happened at each of our several meetings during the next week. We decided whatever had caused this weird experience must not be harmful, since nothing bad had happened to us. Therefore, we jacked up our courage and returned to the butternut tree.

Immediately, we felt the calm, relaxed feeling under the tree. We just stood there for a minute or so before we started talking. This time we had just a quick review of our actions of the past week to run through our minds. We could think of no logical explanation for why both our minds would react as they did, but it was no longer scary. Relaxing under the butternut tree for a few minutes allowed us to forget the anxieties of our teenage lives.

We both returned to this tree often over the next few years until we both left our homes to seek our destiny in the world. I did not feel compelled to go visit the tree but enjoyed going back there to have a relaxing moment.

Without my friend, I sought out another butternut tree a

few miles away and stood under it for a while. The same calmness and tranquility came over me but my mind did not review my life's recent events.

After I left West Virginia, I did not think of my butternut tree encounters until many years later. When I recalled the weird episode under the tree, I developed a theory to explain what happened. You might suspect the many science fiction books I have read heavily influenced my theory, but I challenge you to come up with a better theory to fit the facts.

Butternut trees are widely scattered and I believe they must be receiving and transmitting stations for aliens from another world. I suspect the aliens brought them here long ago. Alien communications equipment is expected to be far advanced over our technological level. Our best instrumentation could never detect them.

The aliens are studying the evolution of our Earth by monitoring the lives of the creatures that wander under the trees. The Horse that stood under the butternut tree would have been a good recorder of everything happening each day on the farm. Each time he returned to the tree, his memory zoomed out to the alien historians. The total relaxation experienced by the horse would lure him back there often.

My theory concerning butternut trees remained plausible until about 1967 when a disease called butternut canker struck the trees and made them an endangered species. Many of them are dead already and all will be gone before long if we cannot stop this dangerous fungus. Anyway, I had to develop a new theory about the trees.

After scratching my head and thinking for a while, this is what I decided was the cause of the butternut trees dying. They were not longer useful to the aliens.

For many years most of America was a rural society and most human and animal inhabitants were often near butternut trees. By the early nineteen sixties, we had become an industrial society. There were many fewer animals and most people now lived in large cities where no butternut trees could grow. The aliens must have introduced the butternut tree canker to dispose of their no longer used communications equipment.

So how do those little guys from distant worlds know what is going on down here now? It is reasonable to expect that aliens are still curious about what we do here.

If I had to guess, I would say the rose bush is the new spy. Most people in cities and rural areas keep rose bushes in their yards. They often stand near their roses to admire them for several minutes, bending over to smell the flowers. Being around beautiful roses does tend to relax people.

If you cannot believe this tale, perhaps you can believe I once loved to eat butternuts and now have many rose bushes in my yard.

HERBAL MAGIC

Walking along the creek bank that ran past my home with my Grandfather is one of my oldest and fondest memories. Grandfather watched honeybees that flew to the creek for water. He noted the angle they traveled when they flew away. After observing several bees from different locations along the creek, he was able to pinpoint the location of their beehive tree on the side of the mountain. Grandfather found many honeybee hives in trees this way and harvested the honey.

I was interested in his running commentary about everything we observed along the way. Grandpa seemed to have an encyclopedic knowledge about everything in nature.

Some family members believed Grandfather had a tendency to exaggerate. They suspected he was too creative in many of his stories. Some of my family doubted his claim to be a good friend of the outlaw Jesse James' brother, Frank James. I wanted to believe all he told me was true.

Some of Grandfathers best stories were about plants and herbs that grew along the creek bank. He claimed the Indians, and early settlers who learned from the Indians, were rarely sick because they knew the herbal remedies. Pointing to a plant along the creek bank, Grandpa would tell me its common name, then tell a story about how it was used it to cure someone of an illness.

I remembered the names of those plants for a long time and could identify them. I have forgotten most of them now because I have not seen the plants for many years. I often wish I had written down the information he gave me but it did not seem as important to me then as it does now.

Recently, I came across a book on herbs and herbal medicine and it brought back an old memory of someone else I had met while a teenager. She was an expert on herbs and had met my oldest brother in a strange way connected to herbs.

The story I will tell you here happened the summer I was fourteen years old. I preferred to fish with friends but none were available to go with me that day. I went to the river alone, seeking fish and adventure.

I had discovered earthworms thrived on decaying cardboard and paper and was able to get a can full from our garbage dump in just a few minutes. My plan was to fish in the New River Gorge where Mill Creek empties into the river.

I did not have a rod and reel for fishing. All I had to carry on the walk down the mountain path was my bait worms, fishhooks in a matchbox and a spool of fishing line. I kept a sharp lookout for a straight tree limb to make a good fishing pole. Near the bottom of the mountain, I found and cut a fishing pole from a tree limb, for which I had great hopes.

A small bridge spanned Mill Creek where it joined the

river. About fifty yards below this bridge was one of my favorite fishing spots. There was no one else fishing there when I arrived. I found a small river rock the right shape to tie on my line for a sinker, and then began to fish.

Previous years experience had taught me bluegills gathered for spawning where I was now fishing. I caught seven bluegills within thirty minutes and was delighted. Two of them were the biggest I had ever caught. The largest bluegill was eleven inches and the other, nine inches in length. After the fish finally quit biting in my hot spot, I decided to walk up Mill Creek and fish the holes between the white water of the stream.

Lower Mill Creek may be the roughest stream to fish in West Virginia. The last half-mile of it before it reaches the river is in a deep canyon with very steep sides and has many huge boulders to impede one's path. I was doing very little fishing, since I could not get any fish to bite in the few spots where I could get near the water.

I believe pollution from a coalmine on Mill Creek may have killed off most of its fish. I never knew of anyone else even trying to fish there.

I finally gave up on fishing in Mill Creek, climbed a steep embankment to the railroad tracks and started towards home. A little ways down the railroad track from me, I saw some people.

There had been several hard rains during the past week. The rains caused many small trickling streams to flow off the mountain above the tracks. At one of the larger of these trickles of water sat an old woman and two small girls. The girls appeared to be about ten and twelve years of age. I would guess the old woman's age to be between sixty-five and seventy-five.

The oldest girl showed an interest in my fish, which I naturally interpreted to be an interest in me, so I stopped to talk for a few minutes.

After they had admired my fish, I asked, "What are you looking at on the embankment by the tracks?"

The oldest girl gestured towards the old woman and replied, "This is my Grandmother, Mrs. Layton. She is teaching me and my cousin about the herbs you see growing here."

Mrs. Layton decided to explain and said, "I was trained in herbal medicine as a child by an older woman with much knowledge of herb use. I want to pass on what I know to the younger generation. There has been an herbal medicine woman in my family for as long as anyone can remember."

I recognized the plants they were observing as rather common around mountain streams but I could not recall their names. The old woman pointed to the growing plants and said, "I call these memory plants. I planted them here because the water draining from this mountain in wet weather contains special minerals, which increase the potency of my memory plants. Some minerals found in water affect potency of herbs and I found this spot is ideal for my memory plants. I have many plantings of different herbs at special streams of water I have found over the years.

"Elderly people who are having memory problems use this herb to keep a good memory as long as they live. It is very potent when made into a tea. You should never use more than one leaf per cup of tea. Never take stronger doses because this herb can do strange things to your mind."

Mrs. Layton asked my name and where I lived and I told

her. She looked surprised and said, "I know your father and oldest brother. I met your brother at this very spot several years ago.

"I came here that day to gather herbs when your father and oldest brother walked by, returning from work in the Mill Creek coalmine. They were both black from coal dust so I knew they were miners. While I was talking to your father, your brother pulled off a twig of the memory herb and chewed several leaves. I would have stopped him but he had already chewed most of it when I noticed what he was doing. I did not know what effect chewing the leaves might have. I had only used the memory plant to make tea.

"The change I expected might happen to him would not be outwardly noticeable. Chewing the leaves could cause one to know about things before they happened and, perhaps, to know what happened at places far away."

Then her eyes got a distant look and her conversation became somewhat far-fetched.

Mrs. Layton continued, "Unfortunately, I took the memory plant in too strong a dose when I was younger. It has caused me to have mind interactions with certain other people. I knew and felt what another person was experiencing when they were under extreme stress. I also foresaw stressful experiences in their future.

"Your brother is one of those I interacted with mentally ever since I met him right here in 1941. He has experienced some stressful moments I have shared since we first met. I was sharing his thoughts when he was on an army troop ship that was torpedoed and sunk."

I was surprised, but figured she could have heard of this incident in my brother's life from anyone who knew him.

Some of her family, at that time, still worked with my Dad at Mill Creek mine.

Then she said, "I now foresee that your brother will soon have a bad accident in the coalmine where he now works."

I refused to believe her. I said good-by to her and the cute little girls and headed home.

When my brother had his hips crushed while working at his coalmining job a few years later, I remembered her prediction. I thought her prediction was most probably a coincidence. Predicting a coal miner will have an accident is a safe bet. Many of my neighbors died or received injuries in coalmines.

I thought no more about my encounter with the old herbal woman and never mentioned it to anyone else. I did think of it sometime later when I was on a fishing trip with my brother at his riverside cabin on New River.

I took my fishing equipment and walked up the river from the cabin to try my luck from a large boulder situated on the riverbank. There was a trickle of water running by the boulder from recent rains and as I sat there fishing; I noticed one of the memory plants growing within my reach. My curiosity about the old woman's claim for this plant drove me to pull off a leaf and put it in my mouth. As I chewed it, there was a mild sour taste with a slight meaty aftertaste.

I gazed into the edge of the river as I considered the taste. I was looking at a piece of log partially submerged in the mud near the bank. It was in an advanced state of decay and there were reeds growing from a spot on it near a knot. There was a small bluegill fish on one side of the reeds and a small bass fish on the other. A frog was trying to hide beneath the tails of the fish.

The reason I have told so many details about my little scene at the edge of the river is, ever since then, I can recall ever detail down to the tiniest pebble. I cannot help but believe my clear recall of that scene from so long ago is only possible because of the memory plant leaf I chewed. If chewing one leaf caused this for me, I wonder what affects the several leaves my brother chewed, leafs with increased potency by the special minerals, might have brought about.

Could he have mental powers of which he is unaware? Perhaps he is aware but does not reveal what passes through his mind.

I have recently taken up woodcarving as a hobby. I have carved the little underwater scene stamped indelibly in my memory. The carving is faithful to what I saw, only limited by my lack of skill as a wood carver.

TRIBUTE TO DAD

I loved to fish and often did so until I left home after high school. I had special spots in the New River gorge in West Virginia where I went for each type of fish I wanted to catch. I caught many bream type fish with most of these being bluegills and sun perch.

My father loved to eat fresh fish of any kind and especially bluegills. I often took home a dozen or more and we would clean and cook them. All my family ate the fish, but for Dad, they were a special treat.

Dad's ability to eat the fish, or any solid food, was rather amazing because he had no teeth. He had not a single tooth. Dad would scrape the meat off the bones so there were no big pieces and proceed to eat with gusto.

I believe the reason Dad had no teeth was just one of the reasons he was the greatest father anyone could have. I want to tell you some things about this coalminer.

My father was born In October of 1896 in White Sulphur Springs, West Virginia. He and his family soon moved to the coalmining region along New River in West Virginia. He quit school and started work in the coalmines when he was nine years old. Dad remained a coal miner until silicosis forced him to give up mining.

Silicosis is a disease miners get from breathing the dust in the coalmine air that contain silica particles. These particles result from the mining process and are worse in certain mines. Silicosis is always fatal and brings about a slow death.

My mother and father had eleven children. They only raised nine children because two died as infants. There were six of us boys and three girls.

Dad served in the army during WWI. Three of his sons served in the army and navy during WWII. One son was a marine during the Korean conflict and the youngest two sons served in the air force and were in Vietnam. All three daughters married men who served in the military.

Until I was ten years old, we lived in a house with no electricity and no running water in the house. We carried buckets of spring water to the house for drinking and cooking. Outdoor "out-houses" were our bathrooms. We took weekly baths in a zinc washtub with water heated on the cooking stove. Mom also heated water for the tubs and washed all our clothes by hand on a scrub board. She finally got an old electric washer with the rollers on top after we moved in 1948 to a house with electricity.

Before dad had to quit the mines because of Silicosis, a typical day for him was to walk three miles each way to Mill Creek mine where he worked eight hours loading coal for thirty-seven cents a ton. When he arrived home, if mom had washed clothes by hand that day, he would cook supper. If it were summer and gardening season, he would work in the garden for a while. I have seen him use his mine lamp mounted on his mine cap to work in the garden after dark.

Dad's only income after his health made him leave the mines was from short jobs he could manage with his short-windedness. Three of us children were still in school, so money was always short.

We never considered ourselves poor. Mom and dad canned all our vegetables from the gardens he raised. We also had chickens and hogs. When the smallest children were still nursing, we also kept a cow. None of us was ever hungry. We wore cheap and plain clothes but they were always neat and clean.

Dad was a great communicator and explained everything we were doing whether fishing, working in the garden or butchering a hog. I have set up well past midnight many nights talking with dad.

We never had a TV while I was home. Dad read the daily newspaper completely every day. He could discuss anything and understood the world situation better than most. Friends and neighbors often asked for his opinion on many matters.

Dad's silicosis disease progressed to the point his lungs would periodically collapse and we had to rush him to a hospital. We thought each time we were losing him. Dad lived several years longer than his doctors had predicted.

After Dad was diagnosed with silicosis, his teeth became a problem so he had them all pulled. Dad decided not to get a set of false teeth because of the cost. He told me he knew his life would soon end and the little money he had available would best be spent on us children.

I often think of my father chewing the fish with his gums and his many sacrifices for his family. He was a great father and a good man, my dad.

FAMILY GHOST STORIES

I remember many of my families stories told in my early years. Those were the days before television when families often gathered in the evenings and talked to one another. We gathered on the front porch on summer evenings and at the kitchen table during the winter.

Mine was a close-knit family and we discussed every subject that any of us brought to the attention of our group. The conversations at these sessions were mostly about mundane matters of little interest to anyone outside the family. However, Dad sometimes told of unusual family happenings and ghost stories.

One of Dad's ghost stories, that I recall well, concerned the events surrounding the greatest coalmine disaster ever to happen. It was in West Virginia. First, I must tell you a little about Dad, since he was associated with coal mining all his life.

Dad quit school in the fourth grade and started work in a coalmine. You may think he was too young to start work, since he was but nine years of age. The use of child labor was common in 1904 when this happened.

The first job Dad worked in the mine was as a gate boy. There were many gates in the mines to direct airflow from large fans on the outside of the mine. All the drift mines had parallel shafts with cross shafts cut between the main tunnels. The gates routed the air to the locations where miners were currently working. Ponies towed the cars loaded with coal from the mine and the empty cars back inside the mine. Dad's first job was to open and close the air gates whenever the ponies approached. It was not long before Dad had advanced to the higher paying job of loading coal into the cars. All miners back then were paid by the ton for coal they loaded.

The Monongah coalmine disaster happened on December 8, 1907. Dad was thirteen years old when this worst ever mine disaster occurred. The mine exploded from the ignition of a large amount of methane gas. The initial explosion was huge. Pieces of mine ponies flew out of the mineshaft, across a river and into the limbs of trees there. Three hundred and sixty-one miners died in the initial explosion and from the poison gas it left in the mine afterward.

Soon after the Monongah mine tragedy, Dad heard a story about a mine inspector that worked in the Monongah mine until three days before the explosion.

Back then, most mines worked one or two shifts. The late shift was used only by the mine inspector to check on safety matters, such as correct post setting to support the roof and other safety concerns.

This unnamed inspector entered the Monongah mine and was doing his job, when he heard a tapping sound. There was not supposed to be anyone else in the mine but him at the time. Thinking someone was working that night that he did not know about, he walked in the direction of the sound.

The sound led him through a cross shaft, over into the main airshaft. He directed his lamp down this shaft towards the sound.

The inspector was shocked and frightened by what his lamp revealed. A few feet down the shaft he saw a black man, dressed in red flannel underwear, sitting on a powder keg. The black man was staring towards the wall of the shaft and was pointing to the outside with his left hand. With his right hand, he held a railroad spike. He was using the spike to tap on the powder keg. The inspector hollered at the man but he never answered but kept tapping on the keg and pointing to the outside of the mine.

The inspector said he immediately quit his inspecting work and left the mine. He believed what he had seen was an omen of something bad to happen in the Monongah mine. He informed his boss of what he had seen and told him he would no longer work in this mine. His boss asked him not to tell other miners. He was afraid they would all quit. The inspector promised he would only tell a relative of his who worked there.

The mine inspector and his relative were the only miners who were aware of the ghost seen in the Monongah mine. Both of them were seeking another mining job three days later when the mine exploded and killed all three hundred and sixty-one miners inside.

Another story about an omen Dad told concerned something strange seen by his mother and sisters. Grandmother and her daughters had just returned from church one evening and were sitting in the living room discussing the church service. Suddenly, they saw a dog with a very long neck sticking its head around the corner from the hallway. Grandmother hollered, "Shoo" and the dog disappeared.

One of my Aunts mentioned that the dog's neck was too long. She did not think it was their dog. They searched the house and could not find their dog or any other. One Aunt then remembered she had locked their dog in an outside shed before going to church. They checked, and their dog was still in the shed. They all agreed the neck of what they had seen was far too long for any dog.

A few days after they saw the long necked dog, one of Grandma's sons died in a hunting accident.

My Grandpa on my dad's side of the family was a very creative storyteller. My Mother felt most of his stories were entirely his creations. Some others in my family believed he was truthful. I will now tell you a few of his stories and let you decide.

Grandpa told of a friend that he hunted wild game animals with on occasion. One day he asked his friend if he would like to hear sounds of something he could identify but which he could not see. His friend agreed and Grandpa took him at night to a certain field not far away.

The location of this field was where a battle occurred during the civil war between the north and south. Back then a section of the main road through this area passed through this field.

Grandpa claimed he and his friend sat near where the old wagon road once existed. Soon they heard sounds in the distance. They heard a horse drawn wagon driven at high speed. There were shouts of the driver to his horse team, the crack of his whip and the clinking of the harness chains. They heard all the sounds you might expect to hear from a wagon driven at maximum speed.

The sounds increased in volume as the wagon neared them and decreased as it passed where they sat. From the sound, the wagon passed within a few feet of them. Neither of them ever saw anything.

Grandpa and his friend left the field and went home. As they were leaving, Grandpa asked the man if he wanted to go hunting again the next day. The man replied, "No thanks, you are too spooky, man."

Another story Grandpa told me concerned bears. My Dad and I were visiting Grandpa and I noticed a bearskin displayed on his wall. I asked him if he had killed the bear. Hear is the bear story he told me.

Grandpa said he and several neighbors were preparing for winter and needed to gather firewood. They harnessed a team of horses to drag trees home then searched nearby woodlands for some dead and seasoned trees.

Grandpa found a large Oak tree that was long dead with the top gone. He knew this would make good firewood. Wondering if the tree snag was hollow, he took his axe and made one hard chop at the tree trunk.

What he did not know was the tree was hollow and had a large opening on the other side from where he stood. A mother bear and two cubs were using the hollow tree as a den. When the axe chopping against the tree disturbed the bear, she was angered and came charging out at Grandpa.

Suddenly appearing before Grandpa was the charging bear, only a few feet away. He let his survival instinct take control and swung the axe as hard as he could at the bear's head. The bear died on the spot. The skin on the wall was from that very same bear.

The story did not end there. Grandpa said they took the two bear cubs home. They gave one cub to a Zoo and the other to a neighbor.

Within a year, the neighbor's cub was a full-grown bear. This man kept the bear chained in his yard and claimed it was tame and a good pet.

One day the young daughter of this man helped in picking the feathers from and cutting up a chicken for dinner. She took the chickens insides and other bloody waste parts, wrapped in a paper, and walked through the yard to where she would dispose of the bloody mess.

Unfortunately, she walked within the reach of the bear on his chain. The bear smelled the blood and attacked her. The bear killed her before anyone could stop it.

Grandpa's wife also told an omen-like ghost story. Grandma died before I was old enough to know her, so I can not swear this is truly her story and not another of Grandpa's.

Grandma was hanging clothes she had just washed on a clothesline. She was in her back yard and her daughter was helping. They lived by a winding river and a railroad track followed the course of the river.

Grandma heard some people singing far away. She said it sounded like singing in Church. She looked in the direction of the sound and saw a group of people walking towards her on the railroad tracks.

The people she saw were carrying a full size coffin with a small coffin on top of it. They were singing as they walked. She watched as the group approached her until they went out of sight because of the bend in the river and railroad track. The people would be very near her when they reappeared from the curve.

They never reappeared. No other path existed they could have followed. Within a few weeks of this sighting, Grandma lost a son due to a hunting accident and a two-year-old granddaughter to pneumonia. The baby who died was my sister and Dad and Mom's first child.

Dad told another ghost story about one of the mines up the river from where he worked. The owners of the mine were not local people and did not know much about the local area. They did know, after a certain date, all the men they hired to pull the mine cars loaded with coal from the mine quit after the first shift they worked. Work at the mine ceased until they could hire an engine operator who would stay on the job.

The owners sent an investigator to interview three engine operators who quit and find out why. All three told the same story.

Their first shift in the mine went fine as they used the engine to drag empty coal cars up to where the miners were loading them. After they connected to the cars that were loaded, they started towards the outside.

There was a long, fairly steep grade of the track inside the mine. This was because the miners must follow where the coal seam leads them. The engine operators claimed that when they reached the bottom of this slope, a woman climbed upon the engine near them and stood on a large crowbar that lay on the floor. When the operators reached the top of the slope, the woman hopped off and disappeared into the darkness. They quit their job as soon as they reached the outside.

The investigators talked to the local Sheriff and he told them who he thought the woman was. During a time when this mine was not operating, someone had taken a local woman on the mine's engine deep into the mine then raped and murdered her. He found her body, after much searching, by the side of the track at the bottom of the steep slope. The killer had clubbed her to death with the crowbar on the engine.

The mine owner's investigator assisted the Sheriff and they solved the crime and arrested the perpetrator. The woman appeared no more to any engine operator and the mine reopened.

MY KOREAN DILEMMA

Most everyone has heard of serial killers such as the Green River Killer and the Zodiac Killer. The Zodiac Killer no longer kills in the Los Angeles area but may be killing elsewhere because he remains unidentified. They caught the Green River Killer and he confessed to forty-eight murders. Both of these men, and many others, have specialized in murdering prostitutes.

Serial killers are different from mass murderers. The mass murderer has a sudden onset of insanity and kills until police arrest or kill him. Their crime spree does not usually last long. The serial killer is someone that blends in with society. These killers arouse no suspicion because they have no visible mental symptoms. They believe their victims deserve to die. Many serial killers continue to kill for years. There are several still killing out there, their identity unknown. I believe I knew a serial killer many years ago in Korea.

I pulled a one-year tour in South Korea while serving in the U. S. Air Force. Like most of the U. S. Bases in S. Korea, there was a small Korean village just outside the main gate of my base. The Koreans living in these villages either worked on the military base or had a business that catered to the

American military.

The business there with the largest number of employees was the oldest profession, prostitution.

I visited several Military Bases during the year I was in Korea and each had their own village or town with the same types of businesses. There were many Bars where the American guys and business girls met, socialized and bargained. All of these young Korean women spoke some English, from very basic to fluent.

The vast destruction of Korean society and infrastructure by the Korean War was still evident when I arrived there. The Korean society I came to know was backward and primitive compared to America and the European countries I had visited. Most of the highways were unpaved and most Koreans lived in very small huts. All the Koreans I met were very hard workers and determined to better themselves and rebuild their country.

I was not married when I was in Korea. Much of my off-duty time there I spent in Bars talking with the working girls. I was surprised to learn very few of them had chosen to work at prostitution.

The Korean society of that era did not value females as highly as males. Poor Korean parents often sold young daughters to owners of prostitution businesses. Their daughters sold for a few hundred dollars. The girls were required to sell themselves and repay the money their parents received before they could work elsewhere. Repayment was made difficult because the Bar owners charged them exorbitant prices for room and board. The situation that many young Korean girls were stuck in was a form of slavery.

A common way out for them was to make an agreement

with an American military man. The American would pay off the girl's debt to the Bar owner and pay all her expenses for the length of his tour. In return, she would be exclusively his mistress. When her American went home, the girl would quickly find another and make the same arrangement. A few of them married American military men.

I talked with many of these girls in Bars near American Bases. Every one said they hated what they were doing and would jump at any chance to get other work.

Soon after I arrived in Korea, I learned many prostitutes were found murdered during the last few years. The Korean and American military authorities did not seem to be expending much effort to find the killer. Most of the girls I talked with knew one or more of those murdered. All the girls were terrified and never went out alone.

There was a young Korean man who owned two Bars in the village I most frequented and more in another village. I met and talked with him several times while visiting one of his Bars.

Orphaned by the War when he was a teenager, an American military unit had taken unofficial responsibility for this young Korean and provided for all of his needs. When his benefactor's unit rotated, another took over his care. He remained close to Americans even as an adult. He spoke American English with no accent and used many American slang expressions. I will henceforth use the alias, "Chang," to identify this man.

Chang was very popular with Americans and I often saw him on the Military Post. I think the top brass must still have been trying to fill in as his family. The one sour note I noticed about him was his evident dislike of his bargirls. When he spoke of the girls, he would usually call them bitches or whores. These girls were vital to business in all his Bars but, for some reason, he hated them.

I was socializing with the girls in a Bar not owned by Chang when several girls discussed the murdered girls. During their discussion, they suddenly became aware that all these dead girls had worked at one or another of Chang's Bars. They became rather excited about Chang's connection to the crimes and decided to inform the local Korean Police. They went to the Police station there in the Village, so I do not know what they said or the reaction from the Korean Police. I heard later that one of the girls informed the American Military Police as well.

Several weeks passed and nothing came of the clues given the Police by the girls. I doubted investigators seriously questioned or investigated Chang because he was one of the local elite.

Another prostitute found dead in an alley near a Base thirty miles from mine caused some excitement among the bar girls. The cause of death was strangulation, like all the others. I knew Chang had a Bar in that Village.

The new murder only got casual attention from the authorities, Korean and American. Their attitude seemed to be, "After all, it was just a whore." I had strong suspicions about Chang's involvement with these deaths. He reinforced my suspicions every time he cursed and berated one of his bar girls. I could think of no way to prove or disprove his guilt in the serial murders.

I lived and worked at a detached site on one base in Korea but my home squadron was thirty miles away on another Base. I drove a military truck because I had to make frequent trips between these two bases. I was late one evening returning to my base so it was after midnight when I drove through the village where I frequented the Bars. Since there was a midnight curfew in effect, there was no activity on the street.

A motion off to my right suddenly caught my attention. I quickly looked that way and clearly saw Chang standing in the mouth of an alley. He quickly jumped back into the alley's darkness. I thought no more about it and proceeded to drive through the main gate to the base.

The next evening after work, I stopped at the Military Club on the Base for a quick beer. I was surprised to hear they had found another strangled prostitute in our village. After dinner, I decided to go to the village and learn the details of what had happened last night.

The girls in my favorite bar were nervous and upset. They all knew the girl killed and that she worked for Chang. When I asked where the body had been found, the girls described the same alley I had seen Chang at last night. I no longer doubted that Chang was the serial killer.

Now I had a large problem. I was positive I saw Chang last night in that alley. However, there was no streetlight there and I only saw him by my truck's headlights. Would the police believe my identification?

I returned to my Base and promptly reported what I had seen to the Military Police. After questioning me, the Police seemed skeptical that it was Chang.

Well, I had done all I could do to get justice for the murdered girl. On second thought, was there something more I could do? Chang was sure to kill again if not stopped. The girls he was killing were barely surviving in a bad situation over which they had no control. They were not prostitutes by choice. Should I take some action?

The next time I visited the Bars in the Village, I discreetly asked a few questions and found out the where Chang slept nights. He had a room for himself with a sleeping mattress in each of his two Bars. He spent the night in whichever bar he happened to be at closing time.

A month later, Chang still had not been arrested for the girl's murder. I had waited long enough. I stopped by the Base whiskey store and bought a bottle of cherry brandy. I went to the Village and killed time until about two hours before the Bars mandatory closing time. Chang had two Bars in this Village and I went searching for him. He was in the first Bar I checked.

I knew some girls working in these Bars had rooms in the back provided by the owner. I asked a few questions and found one girl who had a room in the back of this Bar. I arranged to spend the night with her after the Bar closed in about an hour.

I had carried my bottle of cherry brandy in a paper bag and now brought it out and offered her a drink. Cherry brandy is a very sweet drink and high in alcohol but not strong tasting. I have never met any woman who did not love it. My date was no exception and had several drinks in the next hour. She was quite drunk when the Bar closed. We retired to her room and, on the way, she pointed out Chang's room for me.

I insisted we have a few more drinks of the brandy before going to bed. She gladly poured us drinks in her glasses. Not a lot of time passed before she passed out. I undressed her and put her in bed.

I waited two more hours before I left her room for a short time. I soon returned and joined her in bed. I was unable sleep that night. I arose early the next day, returned to the Base and went to work.

When I returned to my barracks the next evening after work, everyone was talking about the death of Chang. Someone discovered his body in an alley two doors away from one of his Bars. He had been strangled the same as all the girls found killed. The next day, the Military Police called me at work and asked me to stop by their office.

I told them where I was the night Chang was killed. They asked if I had heard anything suspicious that night. I explained that my date and I drank too much and passed out. We heard nothing.

There were two other girls with rooms near Chang's that were questioned by Korean and Military Police. These girls confirmed my story and said they heard nothing suspicious that night. The Police suspected the same killer murdering the girls had murdered Chang.

Three years later, I talked to a Sergeant recently returned from Korea and he told me no more bar girl were murdered after Chang died.

Thinking back about that time in my life, I now recognize the moral dilemma I faced then. The dilemma remains; can two wrongs ever make a right?

I MET BIGFOOT

A large ape/man creature is frequently seen around our world. These creatures look alike but have different names, depending on their locale. Some of these names are:
- The Abominable Snowman—Asia
- Yeti—Asia
- Sasquatch—North America
- Bigfoot—North America
- Skunk Ape—Florida, USA
- Yowie—Australia

The name "Sasquatch" is an American Indian word meaning, "furry man." Sasquatch was part of American Indian lore long before Europeans arrived in America.

Reports of seeing the ape/man creature itself are rare, although its tracks show up more often. The tracks are larger than a man's footprint and noticeably much wider. These tracks are always of a bare foot, even when found in snow. Therefore, I prefer to call this creature Bigfoot.

Some sighting reports of both Bigfoot and his tracks are outright lies. Several instances of people creating tracks and filming someone costumed to appear as Bigfoot were exposed. The reports of sightings that seem legitimate and no one could disprove are numerous. Many who have studied these reports believe the creature is real.

Reports of how the creatures look vary little. Bigfoot's observers described him as seven to nine feet tall, covered with reddish-brown hair, and a body shape somewhere between man and ape. In some areas, Bigfoot has black fur. The face is ape-like except its eyes, which are more like ours.

There are no reports of Bigfoot trying to communicate with people in any language. The only sounds heard from it have been animal like howls, grunts and screams.

I read one serious study of the many reports of Bigfoot that concluded they were most likely from another dimension. This theory gains support because many of the creature's tracks suddenly end as if the creature disappeared. The concept that these creatures can venture back and forth from another dimension to ours at will is not widely believed because few can accept that other dimensions exist.

A more plausible theory advanced speculates Bigfoot is a creature devised and controlled by aliens to study our planet. Smart aliens could have used Ape genes for size and strength and human genes for intelligence to create an explorer most suitable for this planet. If you assume that Bigfoot only ventures down to earth for short scouting and study missions, that would explain why there is so little evidence of their existence on earth.

The idea of Bigfoot having a permanent home on our earth is not believable. No creature this large could have lived here so long without being identified and accepted by mankind as a part of our natural environment.

I know the alien scout theory is true because I met Bigfoot one night long ago. My meeting that night was so eerie and unlikely that I decided not to tell anyone. I felt no one would believe me. Now, I am an old man and care little if you do not believe me, so I will tell you exactly what happened.

I was living in Anchorage, Alaska thirty-five years ago and had a friend fly me 130 miles into the wilderness and leave me there. I camped by a stream containing many trout and salmon. I intended to live off the land for a few days. I had all I needed to cook fish I might catch and some dehydrated meals in case my fishing luck was bad.

Many wild game animals were my neighbors at this campsite. I saw several Beavers, Moose, Black Bears and a Grizzly Bear. Grizzly Bears could pose a serious threat to me so I kept my rifle near at hand at all times.

While fishing the stream my first day there, I looked at all the animal tracks. There is a distinct difference between a Grizzly's and a Black Bear's tracks. I found tracks of both. Thankfully, no Grizzly tracks were near my camp. There was one bend in this stream with a rather large sandbar. I found many animal tracks there. I knew what creature made each of these tracks, except for one.

One footprint I saw clearly in the sand made the hair stand up on the back of my neck because it looked like a barefoot human's track. When I compared it to my foot, I could see it was much larger and wider than any human foot could make. This made me quite nervous for a few minutes. I could not believe what I was seeing. Thoughts of the Bigfoot stories passed through my mind.

The fishing was good that day and I soon dismissed the weird footprint from my mind. I tossed all the fish I caught back into the stream except two grayling I kept for my dinner. I traveled up the stream and fished until ten o'clock that evening.

My adventure in the wilderness happened during the month of June. Alaska never gets completely dark in the summer months. A few hours in the middle of the night are less bright but one can read a newspaper without a lamp during the darkest part of the night. I never took an artificial light of any kind on my camping trips.

I feasted on my delicious grayling for dinner then sat by my campfire and listened to the sounds of the night. The sounds I heard in the twilight of the Alaskan night were interesting because I could not identify all I was hearing. I knew I would sleep well listening to the trickling water in the stream. About midnight, I entered my small tent and crawled inside my sleeping bag. I kept my rifle by my side as I slept.

I awakened to the sound of terrible, angry noises in the middle of the night! Noises so threatening I was instantly wide awake and scrambling from the tent with my rifle!

I was camped on a level place by the stream at the foot of a steep hill. The savage noises I was hearing came from maybe twenty yards up this hill. There was sufficient light to see but thick trees and undergrowth blocked my view of the location of the noise. I stood there and listened to what sounded like two creatures in a fight to the death.

I was almost sure one of the creatures in this fight was a bear, even though I had never heard a bear make such savage and distressed sounds. I had no clue of what the bear's adversary might be.

The sounds it made were hoarse yelps, howls and groans. I could hear small trees and underbrush snapping and breaking from the violent confrontation. From the movement of the brush, I could tell the fight was rapidly moving down the hill towards me. I was only a matter of moments before they burst into my view not more than twenty feet from where I stood.

I was right about the bear sounds. The first one I identified was a very large Grizzly Bear. He had his teeth clamped on the leg of his opponent and was dragging him into the open. When he had pulled the creature into my view, I got the shock of my life! I had never seen anything like this animal!

I was looking at a gorilla-like animal but larger than any gorilla I had ever seen. Whatever this might be, it had reddish brown hair. The expression on this animal's face was of pure agony.

After a second look, I recognized what I was seeing. I was looking at Bigfoot in a fight with a Grizzly Bear.

I do not know why, but I immediately decided to take Bigfoot's side. My rifle was at my shoulder and aimed instinctively at the bear. I squeezed the trigger and shot the Grizzly through the head, from ear to ear. He immediately dropped to the ground and never moved again.

I approached Bigfoot cautiously, hoping he would not continue his battle with me. When he saw me, I swear he smiled for just a second. He raised his arm and waved for me to come. As I neared him, I could tell he had serious problems. Open wounds on both his arms and one leg were bleeding badly. There was no sign of his blood clotting and I guessed he would not last long if I could not stop the bleeding quickly.

I rushed back to my tent and grabbed the canvas that covered the floor and my spare shirt. When I started applying pressure bandages to his open wounds, Bigfoot seemed to know what I was doing and sat there quietly. In a few minutes, I was finished and the bleeding was under control.

When Bigfoot tried to stand, he fell back on his rump. Evidently, there was muscle or bone damage sufficient to prevent him using that leg. With great strain and effort, I was able to drag him near my campfire and cover him with what was left of the canvas. There was still a pained look on Bigfoot's face but he seemed less tense now. I looked at this creature and thought, "What in the hell am I going to do now?"

The problem was abruptly taken out of my hands. I heard a swooshing noise and looked towards the sound. I saw a strange creature appear on a level spot between the stream and me. This was a being even stranger than Bigfoot, still resting by my fire.

I was shocked and frightened out of my wits! As upset as I was, I knew I was looking at an alien. This creature before me was not from this earth. About five feet tall, he appeared more mechanical than organic. His body was shaped like a squared off human. His face was oval and was the only part appearing to be made of flesh.

Before I could decide whether to shoot him or run, a voice came from the thing and said, "Relax, I am not going to do you harm. I want to thank you for aiding my damaged scout." The voice sounded artificial and without the normal inflection of a human voice. I was talking to a computer, I felt sure.

Curiosity overcoming fear, I asked him, "Do you control the big-footed creature?"

"Yes. I am part of the control system for this scout. I lost control for a short time when the animal you killed attacked him. Now I will repair his wounds," he said.

He walked to Bigfoot, bent over, and removed the canvas covering and the three bandages I had applied. The wounds were still seeping blood, but not too much. Removing a spherical container from a pouch he carried, this creature manipulated it somehow to spray a liquid on each of Bigfoot's wounds.

The affect of this spray was astonishing! I could actually see the wounds heal! In two minutes or less, the wounds of Bigfoot had disappeared, grown over completely.

"Wow," I said. "I would love to get my hands on some of that medicine."

"Not possible," said the alien. "Your planet is not ready for our advanced technology. The world you inhabit is still extremely backward compared to most other nearby worlds. You humans must reach a certain level of understanding before you will be accepted into the Universal Society."

"Wait a minute! If we are such inferior beings, what are you and your scouts doing here?" I asked.

"Our mission here is to prevent you from destroying your planet and its flora and fauna before you become wise enough to protect it. If you do not show progress in a reasonable timeframe, we will leave and allow this planet to self-destruct. We have been instrumental in preventing you from destroying yourself many times," he declared.

His lack of respect for humans hurt me. However, I knew enough about the damage we cause to our planet to suspect he was being truthful. I decided to find out anything I could that might be helpful to planet earth's advancement.

"Will you tell me how you managed to appear in front of me without any visible means of transport?" I asked.

"Your society's imagination is way ahead of its technology. Several human creative persons have imagined matter beamed across space and reconstituted as matter. Your scientists have yet to duplicate this feat," he said.

"Why not give me a few important clues that I can use to make great advances in our technology?" I begged.

Bigfoot then stood on his feet and walked with the alien to the spot where the alien first appeared. The alien turned back to me and said, "To save your world requires much more than technological advances. Most important is changing human priorities. As long as most humans believe preparing for an unproven afterlife is more important than doing important deeds while alive, mankind will remain doomed to extinction." Just as I heard his last word, the alien and Bigfoot disappeared. I never dreamed it was possible to beam someone up to a starship!

I was unable to fly home for several more days because of the low overcast weather. I dragged the grizzly bear to a low spot and covered him with stones. I did not want to explain why I illegally shot a protected animal. Then I sat by my campfire, thinking about my strange adventure. I decided not to speak a word of it to anyone.

I believe a person's credibility is extremely important for any kind of success. Convincing anyone my adventure in the wilderness really happened, with no proof of any kind, was not likely.

Now that I have told you my story, do you believe in Bigfoot and UFO's?

JUST OUTSIDE ROSWELL

I lived in Clovis, New Mexico for about a year in 1969 and 1970. I was a member of the U. S. Air Force assigned to Luke Air Force Base, just west of the town of Clovis.

Luke AFB had the new F-111 aircraft which used a new variable wing. There were major difficulties with the wing design. Several crashes of the aircraft focused attention on the new wing, so all of the aircraft were grounded. The Air Force and the aircraft manufacturer were working to solve the problem while I sat around, bored to distraction.

My job at Luke AFB should have been repairing the electronic systems on the F-111. Since none of these aircraft were flying, I had no job. Tired of sitting around waiting, I volunteered to be the Squadron Training NCO. Training was easy compared with my normal job, so I had plenty of spare time to pursue off-duty interests.

Now that I am an old man, I do not hunt and shoot wild animals. During my stay in New Mexico, I still enjoyed hunting and shooting, an interest I developed as a teenager. Quail hunting and fishing occupied much of my time off duty time while I was there.

I lived in a rented house on the southern edge of Clovis while at Luke AFB. I soon discovered, through gossip at work, that the state of New Mexico Fish and Game Department had a large property several miles south of where I lived. They had set aside this property to breed quail, which they used to restock other areas of the state. The property surrounding the restricted quail preserve was public lands for many miles. Public lands are open to hunting for anyone with a valid hunting license.

A friend and I discovered several areas near the quail preserve that were thick with quail. The Fish and Game people should have known they could not restrict coveys of Quail to a certain area. These game birds fly wherever they want and ignore containment fences.

I ate quail often in Clovis. Quail are the tastiest of all wild game birds, in my opinion.

My hunting area with all the Quail was between Clovis and Roswell, New Mexico. I bet you have heard of Roswell. You may remember it as the place where the UFO (or weather balloon) crashed in July of 1947.

I have a keen interest in UFO's. I have read all the articles and books about UFO's I could find over the years. The story of the 1947 crash at Roswell and our governments attempt to cover it up was an old familiar story to me.

Initial reports in 1947 by local reporters told of a UFO crash. There were five aliens inside the crashed UFO. The material used to construct the UFO was unlike anything found on earth. It was a metal-like substance, which jumped back to its original shape when flexed and could not be broken or penetrated.

A short time later, the government said the initial report was wrong. According to the official report, a weather balloon crashed at Roswell. They denied recovering five small human-like bodies from the crash. Several people directly involved with the crash investigation and recovery claimed the government lied and the initial reports were the truth.

Soon after the Roswell UFO report, in March of 1948, another UFO crash was reported in Aztec, New Mexico. This UFO had fourteen alien bodies in the wrecked flying saucer. Another government denial and cover up occurred in Aztec.

Two years later in Farmington, New Mexico, there were numerous UFO sightings. These sightings happened on three consecutive days in March of 1950. Many residents of Farmington observed UFO's on each of the three days. Our government did not explain what these people saw in the sky.

I have read much speculation about what might have attracted so many aliens in UFO's to New Mexico at just that time in our history. A common theme for speculation was the attraction of the government's atomic laboratory at Las Alamos and the nuclear bomb experiments there in New Mexico.

There were also reports that it may have been another highly classified project in progress there in New Mexico at the same time. This project concerned man made flying saucers.

Germany's Adolph Hitler had many scientists trying to develop a nuclear explosive device before America successfully did so. Hitler's scientists also had another top-secret project. The reports that leaked out indicate German scientists had circulated a liquid rapidly in a circular path in a certain way. Their discovery generated unimagined power and could even defy gravity. They were in the process of trying to develop a practical application for this discovery when they were defeated in WWII.

If you lived in the years following WWII or studied the history of that time, you know the U. S. government brought many German scientists to this country after the war. These immigrant scientists continued their research here in America. Werner Von Braun was the most well known of these scientists but there were many others working for us in obscurity. This group of scientists played an important role in developing the rockets for our space program, weapon carrying missiles and many other secret programs.

The German project to develop a flying disk was never mentioned after the scientists working on that program came to America. Many of us believe our government pursued the flying disk project. Since many of the German scientists lived and worked near Los Alamos, New Mexico, that was most likely the projects home. No reports have ever surfaced telling if there was any progress in developing a flying disk.

There are some who believe the work to develop the flying disk was the main attraction for the UFO's seen in New Mexico in the nineteen forties and fifties. I learned what it was all about one Saturday during a quail hunting trip in 1970.

My hunting friend phoned Friday evening and informed me he could not go with me to hunt on Saturday. I prefer to bird hunt with a partner for safety reasons. Some who have hunted with me swear the reason for my partner is so I can brag about how many birds I shoot. I made a few phone calls and my other hunting friends were unavailable for tomorrow. I considered staying home and doing chores but finally decided, "What the hell, I'll go alone.

Ten o'clock on Saturday morning I arrived on the open prairie to hunt quail alone. I chose to hunt the area where I had found the most quail last Saturday. I was on public land within site of the main highway going south to Roswell. I did not have a bird dog so I walked in an S shaped pattern over a large area. I soon suspected the Quail there last week must be on vacation, since I did not jump any. About noon, I quit hunting there and went in search of a new location.

I drove a few miles closer to Roswell and turned onto a dirt road that had no sign forbidding me to enter it. I drove for several miles down this bumpy dirt road and the land looked the same for as far as I could see.

The first Spanish explorers to eastern New Mexico named this prairie Ilano Estacado. That term is Spanish for "Staked Plain." Native Indians traveling there drove wooden stakes into the ground as markers to find their way back when they had to cross this flat country. There were no natural landmarks such as trees, streams or mountains.

The military men there told a joke to new arrivals concerning the vast flat terrain. They said if an Airman walked away from duty on our base, he would not be reported AWOL (absent without leave) for a week. The reason given for why not was he would still be within sight.

I found a place on the dirt road wide enough to turn around, so I stopped there to hunt. I started walking my S shaped pattern in the direction away from the dirt road. The loud fluttering sound made by a flushed covey of quail soon surprised me, as it always does. I quickly fired three shots and downed five quail. That was two birds more than usual for three shots. Sometimes, the birds in flight will align themselves in a pattern that is advantageous to the shooter.

Past hunting of grouse and quail has conditioned my reflexes. I cannot avoid jumping a little from the sudden sound of large birds taking flight. I have trained myself to react by jerking my gun up to my shoulder so I am prepared to shoot immediately.

I retrieved my quail and continued my hunt but flushed no more Quail that day. When I turned to go home, I could see my auto as a tiny dot in the distance. That is the moment in time when things got strange.

There was not a cloud in the sky but around me was suddenly a shady spot. A quick glance around showed there were no trees or other source for the shade, as I well knew.

I looked up and there was a round disk blocking the midday sun. I almost went into shock! Round and disk shaped, it was surely a UFO! I watched it slowly drift downward and land very near me. As it neared the ground, I heard a quiet humming sound.

I was too terrified to run! What could aliens want from me?

Looking closely at the UFO, I guessed it would be over one hundred feet in diameter and thirty feet thick at the center. Three legs had extended just before it touched down. As I continued to observe, a small ramp extended down from underneath the center area.

I recalled the stories of the little aliens from the Roswell UFO incident. The being descending the UFO ramp now in front of me matched the description of the dead aliens at Roswell. It was the physical size of a ten your old human but had an oval face with a much larger head.

This alien paused at the bottom of the ramp and I heard a clear voice in my head. It was very eerie. This was not normal sound I was hearing but it was my language and understandable. The voice said, "Please put down your gun. I do not want to be shot."

I placed my gun on the ground and took a few steps away. I was not going to risk making this little guy angry.

The alien approached me and stopped about six feet away. "Relax. I am not here to do you any harm. I wish only to communicate with you."

Unbelievably, I did relax. Maybe it was because he was small and talked friendly or perhaps because of some unknown control he had gained over me.

It was odd how I could hear his voice but his lips never moved. On reflection, I believe he propagated a signal to communicate directly with the part of my brain that translated sound waves for me. In turn, the sound waves of my voice must have passed through some interpreting device to be understandable to him.

"I am part of a group assigned to permanently monitor your planet," he continued. I have been here for fifty of your years. Before I came here, this world posed no threat and we sent occasional scouts to check on your progress. Now I monitor you to keep aware of your development and insure you do not become a threat. I have orders to stay out of your view as much as possible."

"Why do you need to monitor us?" I asked. "You are obviously much more advanced. You can travel great distances through space and we cannot. What do you want from humans?"

"Today, I just want to know what you believe about UFO's and we who are alien to your planet," he replied. "Most leaders on your planet try to convince humans we do not exist. I have now been here fifty years and I wish to know what you believe. I selected you to ask because I monitored your brain activity earlier today and classified you as an average human. Tell me, before you saw me today, did you believe in UFO's and aliens?"

I thought a moment, and then replied, "Yeah, I knew there were some strangers in our neighborhood. I also knew my government does not tell what it knows about you. I think many people doubt you exist because, even though some people say they saw you, you have never introduced yourself. So tell me, just who in the hell are you and what are you doing here?"

The little guy actually smiled! "Okay, I will come clean!" he exclaimed! "Your habitable planet was discovered many millennia ago. Observers often visited you from several nearby worlds. Long ago, with the approval of the Universal World Government, a team came here and genetically manipulated your most intelligent and adapted primate species. Enough of those primates were given a brain more like ours in the Universal Society, to begin your species. Then we just stood aside and watched your world evolve. Our experiment did not work as well as we hoped.

"We mistakenly allowed mankind to retain many of his primitive survival instincts. The new men we fashioned still had trouble recognizing the value of groups outside their tribe. Our creation retained the primitive urge to dominate all others.

As you know, mankind has fought many wars over thousands of years. We have patiently waited for your species to evolve and become more sociable but you still act like a primitive savage too often.

"Our aim has always been to accept you into our Universal Society. We are still waiting for you to meet our minimum standards.

"A crisis developed here during and just after your largest war which you name WWII. Some of your scientists were well on the way to developing a space/time travel machine using the same basic technology as our transports use. We sent a special team from one of our worlds to assess the situation.

"Unfortunately, this team was not totally aware of the existing technology here. You had recently developed a device called radar to track aircraft from a distance. Our assessment team was in great danger because this radar occasionally interfered with our crafts guidance system. Several of our transports, which you call flying saucers, crashed and lives were lost before the problem was discovered and corrected.

"The remaining members of our team did their job and reported to our Universal Government. Our government decided that we could not allow you to have the time/space travel machine because you would become a serious threat to other worlds if you could reach them.

"I am not free to tell you how your flying saucer program was stopped. I ask you to accept that we will allow you to develop this device if you ever become civilized to the point where you pose no threat to other worlds."

I stood there fascinated with my mouth agape like a simpleton. I finally got my thoughts together and asked him, "Is it okay to tell people what you said here today?"

"Sure, you can tell every word. No one will ever believe you. If you write about it as fiction, you could get more people interested." He smiled as he walked back to and entered his flying saucer. Maybe he was just showing off but when he left, his ship suddenly became a blur and then it was gone. I picked up my gun and went home.

Now that you know this story, you can blame the alien genetic foul-up for losing your temper and every time you act like a savage.

BIRTH OF A CYNIC

I was going to France! My cherished dream of traveling all over the world was about to begin!

Three days after I graduated from high school in May of 1956, I enlisted in the Air Force and left home for basic training in Texas. Military basic training is brainwashing designed to insure unquestioned obedience to all orders. I did not enjoy basic training in San Antonio, Texas.

My next assignment after basic training was on the coast of Mississippi. I completed a technical school there to learn Morse code and voice procedures needed to be a Ground Radio Operator. This technical school had an incentive program whereby the student with the highest scores upon graduation, which I had, would receive his choice of assignment afterwards.

I elected to go to France for a three-year tour. France is centrally located in Europe and I hoped to visit all the countries around it. I knew nothing about France except what I had read. I did not speak French or any other foreign language. I was still a few months short of my nineteenth birthday when I got my orders to go. I would ship out in

January of 1957.

There was a military depot in New York City where my orders directed me for transport across the Atlantic Ocean to France. Normally, all Air Force personnel flew back and forth to overseas assignments. The Christmas holidays created a large backlog for all military overseas replacements that year. Due to the large backlog, my transport would be a troop ship.

I had a delay of ten days before my ship departed. I used the waiting time to travel by subway over most of New York City. I visited Times Square and other places that were of interest to me there. I think of my experience there as similar to Alice in Wonderland, except the characters I met in New York were weirder.

One of my life's most memorable moments happened as I sailed out of New York Harbor. My troop ship passed very close to the Statue of Liberty. Many of us military guys stood on deck to view the famous statue as we steamed by. No man-made symbol has ever impressed me more. The awareness I was leaving everyone I knew and would be gone three years made the moment more emotional.

The North Atlantic Ocean is definitely not a calm pond in January. My troop ship was constantly rocking side to side and fore and aft, during the nine days it took to reach port in Bremer Haven, Germany.

In addition to the troop ship's crew, there was about a thousand U. S. Army troops, a few Marines and five hundred Air Force troops on the ship with me. Many troops were assigned work on the ship but they filled all the jobs before my name came up on their roster. I occupied my time by reading or going on deck to look for flying fish while getting a breath of cold, fresh air. Many of the Army guys had a rotating player poker game that lasted the whole trip.

The rough seas caused many troops to suffer from seasickness. I learned just how much the human mind is susceptible to suggestion on several of my visits to the deck. I would be standing with a crowd of maybe a hundred troops with everyone smiling, laughing and pointing to the flying fish. Then, one troop would vomit and everyone there would recognize the sound and smell of it. Within just a few minutes, nearly half of them would vomit. I never vomited although I felt a little sick for most of that voyage.

My troop ship arrived in Bremer Haven, Germany on schedule and I got on a train for Chaumont, France.

The first months of my work at Chaumont AFB taught me I was in a dying career field. Teletype was now the primary means of communications of the military services. There was a mobile van out behind the Communications Squadron building where I worked my shifts, sending and receiving messages in Morse code to other Bases in France and Germany. We radio operators were emergency back up for the Teletype communications.

The worst news was that no promotion was possible in my career field. My Ground Radio Operator career field was phasing out completely. My recent promotion to Airman Second Class was the last promotion I could have until I changed to another career field. I could not change career fields until I rotated back to the States.

The cold war with the USSR was near its peak at that time. Russia was the main threat perceived by the Pentagon during the years I was in France. They anticipated Air Force Bases destroyed by Russia's atomic bombs.

The normal Air Force Fighter/Bomber Base has three

squadrons of aircraft. The strategy of "dispersal of base," called DOB, was initiated. Two sites were constructed far enough from each home base to insure they would not be damaged if the main Base were nuclear bombed. One squadron of the Wing's Fighter/Bomber aircraft flew to each of the two sites during alerts. The idea being, one enemy atomic bomb could not destroy all three squadrons of a Fighter/Bomber Wing. This strategy informed Russia our surviving aircraft would retaliate for any attack with our own nuclear weapons.

The runways were under construction at these DOB sites when I arrived in France. I was among the first assigned to a site on a permanent basis.

There were six of us sent to the site near the small village of Brienne Le Chateau, France. The Base there took the name of this French town but we all shortened the name to Brienne. Three of us were from the Communications Squadron. The others were Air Policemen, assigned to guard supplies and equipment stored at the site.

We lived in a nearby Army housing area at first. The Air Force paid us extra to eat in local French restaurants and we learned about French cuisine. There is where I first ate snails, called escargots in French. Despite my previous view of snails as slimy pests, I really liked their taste.

There were two Air Policemen in our group from Louisiana and who spoke fluent French. We all soon learned enough of the French language to order our food and count in French.

Within a few months, the site at Brienne Le Chateau had expanded to house a larger caretaker crew. A full squadron of aircraft and its people would only come there during an alert practice or an actual alert. I moved into a tent city the Air Force built near where I had been working for several months.

Our population went up to about forty personnel and gradually increased as time passed. We even had our own cooks and a mess hall. I slept on a folding cot in a large tent. For taking a shower, we had a large barrel of water on an elevated platform. There was a rope to pull causing the water to pour down.

They did construct a building with commodes that connected to a sewer line. This toilet's interior was open with no dividers between commodes. Can you picture having a bowel movement with your commanding officer seated on one side and the military chaplain on the other?

Several friends at the Brienne site owned automobiles. A group of us regularly rode with them to spend weekends in Paris or Amsterdam, Holland and twice to Basil and Zurich, Switzerland. A few trips were to parts of Europe more distant but they required a long holiday weekend. Many weeknights we would visit the nightclubs in the nearby city of Troyes. I will not tell here all we did on our many trips. Suffice it to say; European women know how to have a good time.

I remained at Brienne Le Chateau for nearly a year and helped build it into a functioning Base. My job as the radio operator did not take up much of my time, since I only had to make one check-in with the radio each day. My boss kept me busy doing other work.

Several of us communication guys had to run a new cable about a mile and attach it to existing power and telephone poles. I was the one who used the spikes strapped onto my feet to climb the poles and attach the new cable.

The job went well and we were in the process of attaching the cable to the next to last pole. I climbed the pole and screwed a large eyebolt into it at the height for the new cable. I inserted the cable coming from a distant pole and lowered it to the ground so my fellow airmen could pull it up to its desired height between the poles. They started heaving on the cable and pulled a few feet at a time through the eyebolt.

A French high voltage power line crossed the path of our new cable about halfway between our poles. It was much higher than we were routing our cable so we did not consider it a problem.

To understand what happened next, you must picture me on the pole with the eyebolt right in front of my face, the cable making a long sagging dip to the distant pole and two airmen on the ground below, heaving on the cable to get it higher. We needed just a little more height before I secured the cable at the eyebolt.

The next heave on the cable bounced it higher than we believed was possible. It bounced near the intersecting high voltage line above it. There was a huge flash as the voltage arced to our cable. A ball of fire zoomed down the cable and popped loudly as it passed the eyebolt just in front of my face. When my vision cleared, I looked down and both airmen below were on the ground. It was but a few minutes before they were able to sit up. A few more minutes passed before my legs stopped trembling enough for me to climb down from the pole.

There was no Doctor assigned to our Base, but we did have a Medic. He checked us out and said we had no problem except shock. He was a wise man and advised us to take the afternoon off and get drunk. We took his medical advice.

There were American military bases over much of Europe while I was over there. The aircraft pilots required a remote area to practice bombing and strafing to maintain their efficiency. A densely populated Europe had no suitable location for a bombing range. The Air Force solved this problem by leasing an unpopulated section of the Sahara Desert in North Africa from Libya.

Wheelus AFB is located on the Mediterranean coast of Libya near the city of Tripoli. All Air Force pilots stationed in Europe went to Wheelus AFB to practice gunnery and bombing on the nearby bombing range.

When it was my Wing's turn for bombing practice, I went with them. The Air Force wanted a mobile ground radio station to maintain communications with all the home Bases back in Europe. I would be the operator. My boss assured me my assignment would be only sixty days of temporary duty.

The Air Force used the C-119 transport aircraft, called the "Flying Boxcar," for transferring people and supplies between the Bases of Europe and North Africa. Aviation Engineers claimed a study of the design of the Flying Boxcar indicated it should not be able to maintain flight, yet it did fly quite well. It is the only twin engine aircraft which has difficulty staying aloft when one engine quits. I boarded a Flying Boxcar aircraft to fly from Chaumont, France to Libya, N. Africa.

I have flown on a number of commercial Airlines and Air Force transport planes before and after my flight from France to Africa. No parachute was ever given me on any other flight. I trained to jump with a parachute in basic training, so I could use one if necessary.

The ground crew handed each of us a parachute as we boarded this C-119. I learned later that all Flying Boxcar passengers must have a parachute because the aircraft cannot maintain flight for long with one engine. The engines sometimes conked out in flight. The interior of this plane had canvas seats placed along the inside walls since it was not primarily a passenger plane. The center of the aircraft was open to store cargo. The whole rear of the aircraft was chopped off with a large door there which was used as a ramp to load and off-load cargo.

Shortly after take-off, the flight crew allowed us to remove our parachutes and stack them in front of us on the floor. They made a large pile.

I had stayed up too late the previous night drinking beer with my friends. Today I was paying the price and was fighting to stay awake. The stack of parachutes in front of me was very tempting. I asked a flight attendant if I could stretch out on them and he gave his approval.

I suddenly awakened to the loud ringing of an alarm bell, the flashing of an overhead light and people jerking their parachutes from beneath me. I heard people saying we had lost one engine. I was wide-awake then and rapidly strapped on my parachute.

The aircraft floor tilted to one side and we were descending at a steep angle. I could see the waves of the Mediterranean Sea too well out my window. Everyone now had parachutes hooked up to the jump line and we anxiously waited for the crew to open the back door and give the jump signal.

Then we heard, first a sputtering, and then the roar of

the defective engine. We were still in a dive but started to gradually level out. With a sigh of relief, I peered out the window when we finally started to climb again. We could not have been more than fifty feet above the water. The remainder of the flight to Wheelus AFB was uneventful.

Europeans I had met inclined me to think that all societies and cultures are essentially alike. My time spent in Libya introduced me to a culture very different from my own. My experience with the Arab culture alienated me forever from all Arab societies.

There were many Arab men employed to provide services on Wheelus AFB. I lived in one of the many transient barracks there. Native Libyans worked around me every day and I came to know several of them. A large number of these men had a white film on one eye that looked like a cataract.

I was talking one day with the Arab cleaning my barracks. He spoke English better than most of the other Arabs. I asked him, "Why do so many of your people have a cataract in one eye. In my country, only the elderly get cataracts and then they appear in both eyes."

"What you see in some of our eyes is not cataracts," he said. "Many Arab mothers use a burning ember or cigarette to destroy the vision of their male children. They only burn the eye used to sight a rifle or other weapon. Men do not fight in a war if they cannot sight a rifle."

I was shocked to hear so many Arab mothers could intentionally do permanent damage to their son's vision. I was sure no woman I had ever known would do such harm to her son for any reason. This conversation introduced me to the radically different Arab culture.

All newly arrived military personnel at Wheelus AFB were briefed about the dangers when visiting the city of Tripoli. We were all discouraged from going into town, but not forbidden to do so.

One of the beliefs of these local Arabs I thought strange concerned anyone taking their picture. They thought you were trying to steal their soul if you photographed them, especially the Arab women.

Shortly before I arrived in Libya, an American Airman took his camera and went into the city of Tripoli. Other Airmen in town that day later reported he was taking pictures of the Arab women. He did not return to the Base that night.

The gates between Wheelus AFB and Tripoli were closed at midnight because the Base Commander imposed a midnight curfew for Airmen going into the town. When the Air Policemen arrived to open the gates the next morning, they found the Airman who was taking so many pictures the previous day, lying dead in front of the gates.

He died from multiple stab wounds. His testicles were cut off, stuffed into his mouth and his lips sewn together. The Arab authorities in Tripoli said a large group of women killed him in this way because he took their picture. Those murderous Arab women suffered no punishment.

A bad dust storm moved over the Base from the Sahara desert while I was there. The thick dust greatly reduced visibility. Combined with the heat and wind, the storm made everyone miserable. My sixty days was about up and I looked forward to returning to France.

My replacement arrived several days before I was to leave for France. I spent a few days teaching him what he needed to know to do my job. Without my knowledge or consent, this young idiot went into Tripoli the first Saturday after he arrived. Late that evening, the Air Police returned him to his quarters.

The story my replacement told me involved an Arab policeman in plain clothes. It seems they were both sitting in a bar and got into an argument. The Arab policeman arrested him and charged him with several vague offenses. The Arab police notified our Air Police of his arrest and they managed to get his custody.

Our people decided to get this young Airman's butt back to France immediately. He was on a plane leaving the next day. My temporary duty tour was extended for another 60 days. When I finally left that hellhole, I had been there seven months.

I had worse luck than I knew while in Libya. When I arrived back at Chaumont, France, I learned from long delayed letters that my Father and an older brother had passed away while I was in Libya. The Red Cross was unable to locate me when they died. I drank too much the rest of my time in France.

I returned to the states after my tour in France a cynical young man. I now see my early cynicism as armor that protected me from my life's mental bumps and bruises.

Those early years of my life taught me many hard earned lessons. Such as, "know your enemies, value your friends and depend on nobody."

THREE EAGLES SCREAMING

I have always had an affinity for the natural world. The interdependence of all flora and fauna on this earth fascinates me. Except for mankind, earth's creatures only destroy other living things as necessary for food or survival. I admire all plants and animals that share my planet but like some more than others. The many varieties of eagles and hawks have long been among my favorites.

It has always made me happy to observe the raptors but sometimes my association with the natural world has had unexpected results. I will tell you here how eagles have twice lifted my spirit and once probably saved my life.

My Grandmother died when I was eleven years old. Her death was the first I had experienced of someone I knew well. I was a truly forlorn youngster and was having trouble accepting the concept that people just go away forever.

My home was about a mile from the New River Gorge in West Virginia. I often walked through the forest to the edge of the cliffs overlooking the river far below. This cliff top offered me a beautiful view and I went there whenever I could.

About two weeks after Grandmother died, I was still depressed and wanted to do something to distract my grief. I decided to walk to my favorite overlook of the river.

When I stood on the edge of the overlook that day, I was surprised to hear a piercing screech from the sky above me. I had heard no sound like it before. When I looked up, there was a large Eagle circling above me in the blue sky. He gave out two more of his unique screams before flying out of sight up the river.

My grief and depression flew off with him. Something about this majestic bird's defiant screaming at my world below allowed me to rise above my childhood and accept the fact of death as an inevitable end to all life.

My next experience with the Eagle was in Vietnam. I had two good friends killed one night by an enemy rocket attack. I was having trouble going on with work as usual and was deeply depressed.

The road from my barracks to where I worked went by the edge of a large body of shallow water used as a rice paddy. Several days after the death of my friends, I was walking to work when I heard the old familiar scream from the sky above. A large Eagle had been feeding on small fish in the rice paddy. He screamed twice more as he flew off towards the jungle.

The sight of him soaring above and screaming his defiance of life's problems gave me the strength I needed to live with my grief and get on with my life.

The next time I saw an Eagle was here in my backyard.

I had the misfortune to have an aortic aneurysm that ruptured and the emergency surgery required to save my life caused me to be a paraplegic. I had trouble accepting how my life was now limited and changed. I found myself doubting it was worthwhile to continue with my life.

I was sitting in my wheelchair on my backyard patio one afternoon about four months after becoming disabled. Suddenly, I heard again the old familiar scream from above me in the sky. There was the largest bald eagle I had ever seen circling me at a low altitude. He began to fly a wide circle as he climbed to a higher altitude. He screamed twice more in the next few minutes as he climbed until no longer within my view.

The eagle's visit truly lifted my spirit and gave me the strength to get on with my life. Thereafter I quit feeling sorry for the things I had lost and concentrated my life on what I could still do. When I saw that majestic eagle and heard his defiant scream, it reinforced my inner elation with life and gave me the strength to overcome my problems.

I think my empathy with the eagle is due to my recognition that I am but one element in the complex balance of nature on this earth. Each natural element can teach me if I study its strengths and weaknesses. I see God in the natural world around me.

Printed in the United States
201205BV00002B/1-105/P